THE JACK REACHER CASES (A MAN BEYOND THE LAW)

DAN AMES

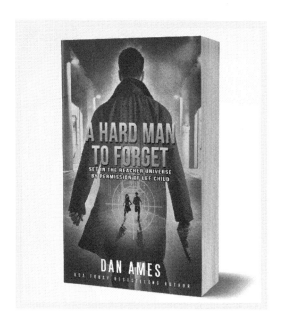

Book One in The JACK REACHER Cases

FREE BOOKS AND MORE

**Would you like a FREE copy
of my story BULLET RIVER and the chance
to win a free Kindle?**

Then sign up for the DAN AMES BOOK CLUB:

THE JACK REACHER CASES

(A MAN BEYOND THE LAW)

BY

DAN AMES

Southern Turkey

The bar was nearly filled to capacity, but even among the densely packed crowd, Jessica Halbert stood out. She was dark-haired with dazzling blue-green eyes and a smile that could melt even the harshest cynic's heart.

It had always been that way. Ever since her beauty blossomed as a young girl, the world had smiled at Jessica Halbert and she had always smiled back. She had one of the utterly honest, positive outlooks on life; a belief that the world was inherently good. And why wouldn't she feel that way? Life, and people, had always been kind to her.

Now she nursed her beer and waited. The establishment was a favorite of the soldiers who were stationed at the nearby army base, less than three miles away. Halbert was one of those soldiers.

On any given night, there were easily a dozen or so Americans drinking hard, trying to make the most of their limited free time, on some level dreading the return to the drudgers that often characterized life in the army. Oftentimes, the tavern was the last stop on the way back from the nearest city for "last call" before heading back to the base.

Tonight Jessica Halbert wasn't returning from time off, she was meeting someone. A person she'd met during their last operation. Things had gotten somewhat interesting between them, and he'd asked to meet her. It was a request she felt she couldn't refuse.

Because she believed in doing the right thing.

That's how the world worked, in her mind.

She was growing impatient, however. A woman who looked like she did attracted a lot of attention in a place like this, and although there were a few familiar faces in the crowd, they were few and far between. The army base was huge and had a fairly high turnover rate of new soldiers rotating in and others rotating out. It meant there was always a fresh supply of complete strangers.

Despite having a full glass of beer, she was repeatedly offered drinks by guys who did double takes after their first look at her. As if she was a mirage in the desert. She politely declined but always did it in a way that made them feel as if she'd been glad they offered.

Jessica Halbert had a way of making people feel happy, even if they didn't get what they wanted. It was as if they didn't win the prize but were pleased to have simply been nominated.

Her phone buzzed in her pocket and she saw that it wasn't a number she recognized. She quickly read the text message and felt a surge of relief. It was her friend and he was waiting outside.

Jessica paid for the beer she hadn't consumed, and worked

her way through the crowd, a few guys not making much of an effort to give her space so they could rub up against her.

Outside, she smiled when she saw the vehicle and climbed inside.

It would be nearly two full weeks before a group of men hunting deer in the deep forest nearly fifty miles from the tavern found the mutilated body of Jessica Halbert.

Gone was the vivacious and warm woman who brought joy to those in her orbit.

In her place was a grotesque corpse that had been beaten, raped, and slashed to pieces in what appeared to be a horrifically violent, frenzied killing.

The local authorities initially handled the case, which turned out to be problematic. They weren't homicide investigators and the crime scene was severely compromised before the army was able to negotiate control of the case.

The first step was to analyze the text message sent to her phone, but it was traced to a disposable burner phone that had gone inactive shortly after the estimated time of death.

Eventually, the case was given to an army special investigator who had an excellent clearance record for difficult cases. He was a big guy, with a physical presence that could unnerve reluctant witnesses or motivate people with secrets to start spilling the beans. He had a love of black coffee and cold logic.

But despite his best efforts and months of intense investigation, the case of Jessica Halbert's murder, much like her body in the army's morgue, went ice cold.

CHAPTER ONE

rmy Medical Center, Virginia

The patient's life hung in the balance, but against nearly all of the doctors' and surgeons' predictions, he continued to survive. They all agreed it was a medical marvel. With multiple fractures, internal bleeding and the near-fatal onset of severe shock, it was astounding the man had survived.

Information on the patient was scant. Previous injuries showed more than one bullet wound, a stab wound, and other signs of a life spent in harm's way.

It wasn't the patient's injuries that garnered the medical staff's first remarks.

No, initial attention was paid to the man's size and physicality.

Being a military hospital, the patient population naturally skewed male. It also exhibited a higher-than-normal percentage of extremely fit individuals. Although fighting men came in all shapes and sizes, the doctors and nurses were used to seeing patients above average in terms of height, width and muscularity.

This patient stood out even among the regulars. He was easily six feet five inches tall, but his arms were longer than normal and his chest and shoulders were nothing short of massive. His pectoral muscles were the size of dinner plates. And his hands were enormous.

The hospital was known to have only two beds that were bigger than normal, and the attending physician had immediately ordered one of them for the new patient.

Even then his large feet hung off the end of the bed, and his shoulders veered over the edge of both sides of the mattress.

A new doctor appeared in the room, with a nurse who'd been one of the attending staff when the patient had originally been admitted.

"What's his story?" the doctor said. His name was Reilly and he carried the air of a man in a hurry who didn't have time to make small talk. "Besides his overactive pituitary gland? Jeez, this guy's enormous."

"Yeah, we had to break out the big bed for him," the nurse said. Her name was Helen and she'd been at the hospital for over five years, which made her an old pro. She had light brown hair pulled back into a ponytail, revealing a flower tattoo on the back of her neck.

"All we know is that it was some kind of car accident," she said. "Maybe a roadside bomb, we don't know. But it was touch and go there for a long time. No one thought he would make it this far. The guy's got incredible stamina and was in incredible physical condition. It's the main reason he pulled through."

Dr. Reilly looked through the chart, which was only a

page and a half. He checked the back of the clipboard as if something was missing.

"This is it?" he asked.

Helen shrugged her shoulders. In a place like this, all kinds of things happened with regards to information and security. A lot of the soldiers who ended up at the hospital were fresh from overseas and security clearances were always an issue.

"I've put in a request for more information, but this is all we have so far," Helen said. "It's unusual, but not unheard of. It all depends on his classification."

The doctor went to the bedside of the patient and checked his pulse, and then used his stethoscope to listen to the man's breathing.

"His next round of meds will be in a few hours," the nurse said. "If you want to speak with him, you'll be the first. He hasn't said a word since he's been here. We don't even know if he can. But he may come around an hour or so before then. He's on enough painkillers now to tranquilize a horse."

"There are horses smaller than this guy," the doctor pointed out.

"Yeah, and he's been ridden hard. Those injuries took some time and lots of pain to acquire. He's a real mystery man."

Reilly nodded and hung the clipboard at the end of the patient's bed.

"It'll be interesting to see if and how this mystery ends," Reilly said. "Let's do our best to make sure it has a happy ending."

He left and Helen went to the patient's bedside and pulled the sheet back up over his chest. The doctor had lowered it to listen to his breathing.

She looked down and smiled at him. He was handsome in a rough-hewn kind of way. Like a rustic log cabin with solid beams that was warm in the winter, but didn't have any fancy touches.

"I'll be back in a couple of hours," Helen said. "Try not to miss me."

The patient's eyes remained closed.

The nurse walked out of the room and when she passed the clipboard, it gently rocked from its hanging position.

At the top of the chart was an empty blank for the patient's name. Next to it, scrawled in pen by hand, was a single name.

In bold.

Reacher.

CHAPTER TWO

The shock hit Pauling full force.

The setting sun cast a crimson light into the room. Lauren Pauling, a handsome woman well north of forty years old, brushed back her light blonde hair, now shimmering gold in the last traces of the day. She caught sight of her reflection in the windows that looked out upon Manhattan, and knew her best features, her green eyes and whiskey-tinged voice, weren't represented in the image.

Now she looked away from the view and back down at the papers in her hand.

She had prepared herself, even taken the proposal home with her rather than reading it at the office. Even though the private investigative firm was her own and she had ample privacy in her own office, some things she liked to keep separate, and it would have almost seemed treacherous to study the proposal within the walls of the firm she was contemplating selling.

The numbers were staggering.

They were much, much higher than she'd expected.

She was glad she hadn't done it at the office as some of

her staff might have noted her shock and wondered what was wrong.

When Pauling had left the FBI after a distinguished career, she'd immediately begun working as a civilian contractor, a private investigator in most cases. Part of the reason she had left the Bureau, ironically, was because she was simply tired of the bureaucracy.

Chasing down bad guys was what drove her, it was the thrill of the hunt.

So moving immediately into working as an investigator in the private sector had been a no-brainer. Eventually, she gained the knowledge and business expertise to open her own firm. She had started small, but her company had grown steadily over the years.

The first offers from rivals who wanted to buy her firm as opposed to competing against it, didn't begin until their clients started departing for Pauling's firm. Their solution was if they couldn't beat her, they'd buy her.

Now a corporate firm that had lost the most business to her and not coincidentally had been her most ardent pursuer, just upped the ante.

Big time.

Pauling took a deep breath and pushed away from the table. She needed to breathe. Her condo was in the middle of what she considered the greatest city in the world, on 4th and Barrow, and featured large windows that looked out over a small park and a section of 5th Avenue.

She'd put in a full day, including a private workout with her trainer over the lunch hour, and now she was tired and flattered.

Should she feel flattered? Proud that someone put that high of a value on something she'd created from nothing?

Damn right I should, she thought.

It was a lot to think about, in every sense of the phrase.

The money was incredible. It was of the I'll-never-have-to-work-again kind. She could travel. Buy a home in Italy. Or France. Or both.

And then what?

As nice as the money was, it couldn't fill her days.

Besides, she didn't want to stop working.

Oh, it would be nice to be free of the administrative and management duties required as a business owner. They were endless.

But give up work?

Pauling knew she didn't want that.

Catching thieves and murderers was in her blood. Her DNA. It's what she did.

The firm who made the offer to buy her out also said she could cherry pick cases to work on, but she knew how that would go. It would be working for someone else. Needing approval. Checking with the higher-ups.

A bureaucracy.

No thank you.

Been there, done that.

Pauling turned from the window, crossed the room back to the kitchen and poured herself a glass of white wine. She turned the offer sheet over so she didn't have to think about it anymore.

At times like this, she often thought of Jack Reacher.

Pauling went into the living room and curled up on the couch. She wondered if she would ever hear from Reacher again.

Little did she know, the answer would be arriving in tomorrow's mail.

CHAPTER THREE

The hospital worker pushed the combination bed/gurney along the hallway, looking every bit the part. His white shirt and pants both bore the official logo of the hospital, and the gurney was clearly medical grade, complete with collapsible sides, and a multitude of levers and knobs for a kaleidoscope of adjustment options.

He wheeled the bed into the patient's room, shut the door and performed the intricate maneuver of rolling the giant man off the bed onto the gurney, using a technique employed by nurses of pulling the sheet in a rolling motion.

Some of the patient's tubes popped from their counterparts and the orderly quickly disconnected a monitor that began to beep.

The patient remained unconscious as he was wheeled through the hallway of the hospital, down to the large elevator and onto the ground floor. The orderly said nothing to the patient. Instead, he hummed a tune that may or may not have been *We Gotta Get out of This Place*, by the Animals.

The patient was whisked through the automatic doors next to the emergency room and into the cool outside air.

It was sunny and clear, but he wasn't able to sense the change in his surroundings. He didn't hear any of the voices around him, nor was he able to see the vehicle he was loaded into.

If he had seen it, the big man would have recognized that something wasn't right. The white van did have the logo of a hospital, but it was only on one side of the vehicle and there were no accessories typical of a medical transport. No bars of red and blue lights that could flash in an emergency. No medical equipment in the back. No aerial antennas for additional communication capabilities.

The rear doors of the van were opened and the collapsible gurney slid onto the floor of the van. It took a tremendous heave from the hospital worker, but he was able to lift the end of the gurney, despite the weight of the big man.

Once the patient was secure, the rear doors of the van were slammed shut and the vehicle drove away from the hospital. No security guards would remember seeing the patient leave the hospital and there were no surveillance cameras filming the area.

The white van with the single hospital logo on one side wound its way through the hospital's campus and then carefully merged onto the freeway where it stayed in the slow lane and made no attempt to speed around slow traffic. Eventually, it took the exit for a road with a sign indicating that it led into the nearby state forest. The sign also indicated there was a boat ramp and campsites were available.

Eventually, the van turned down a dirt road that skirted a small pond. Passing the public access boat ramp, the vehicle instead bounced along a secondary gravel road bordering a marshy area. There, it made a series of turns that steadily led away from any signs of human occupation, in the opposite direction of the camp areas.

Finally, when the last road amounted to no more than a

dim two-track choked with weeds and mud backing up into a stretch of tall grass with soft, mucky earth, it stopped.

There, it carefully executed a U-turn, nearly getting stuck, until the vehicle was facing back toward the trail and its rear doors were several feet from a recently dug pit. During his scouting excursion, the driver had found the remote location and decided to do the hardest work ahead of time, which would also limit the risk of exposure.

The driver exited the vehicle, opened the rear doors and climbed into the rear of the van. From inside his white jacket he withdrew a large hypodermic needle filled with a combination of sodium thiopental, pancuronium bromide and potassium chloride, the triple-strength cocktail most often used in executions performed by lethal injection.

He plunged the needle into the large man still strapped to the gurney. Moments later, the patient was dead.

The gurney with its now lifeless body was pushed from the van and rolled directly into the freshly dug grave, sinking into the watery muck at the bottom of the trough.

The driver's hospital clothes and the hospital logo decal from the side of the van all joined the dead man in his final resting spot. Using the only other item from the van's interior, a shovel, he shoveled mounds of moist dirt on top of the grave. The driver, wearing surgical gloves to avoid leaving prints, then tossed the shovel out into the pond, where it sunk from sight. He would throw the surgical gloves away after he ditched the van.

Satisfied, the driver got back into the now generically white van, and drove away.

CHAPTER FOUR

Michael Tallon had been walking for two days. He wasn't lost. Nor had his car broken down.

For the last 48 hours, he had been recreating a forced march he'd endured nearly twenty years earlier, on one of his first missions. It had taken place in Africa, near the western edges of the Sahara Desert. His team, although he was not in command as he was still a young soldier, had nearly perished. The heat had been brutal and they'd been on the run from a much larger enemy force, with no hope of an extraction.

It had been one of his most physically challenging experiences of his life.

So, naturally, he'd wondered if he could recreate it. Now more than twenty years later. It was the kind of twisted physical challenges men like Tallon often dreamed up to stay fit.

As he and his buddies were fond of pointing out back in their younger years, when the alpha males were constantly eager to challenge each other, things tended to "escalate quickly."

It didn't matter to Tallon that he was much older and that

his body had endured many hardships since that period of his life way back when. There had been broken bones, gunshot wounds, and a rusty bayonet jammed into his thigh, along with the usual bouts of strange illnesses from operating in foreign lands under hostile conditions.

No, Michael Tallon simply didn't believe age had anything to do with physicality. It was all mental. Aging was simply an excuse, in his mind.

So now he swept down the southern edges of Death Valley, the heat well over one hundred degrees, and powered through the final hour of his march, reaching his adobe ranch house just before sundown. He checked his watch, and was disappointed that his two-day excursion had taken him nearly six hours longer than when he'd done it decades ago.

Of course, back then, there had been bad guys with lots of guns chasing him.

A little extra motivation.

Tallon disarmed the extensive security system, went inside and drank deeply from a cold bottle of water. He was exhausted, filthy and extremely pleased the ordeal was over.

He showered, changed into shorts and a T-shirt, and ate slowly from the prepared meal he'd made for himself before he'd left. Just the right mixture of carbs, protein and fat. Not much, though. He would have to ease back into his meals.

Although his body was exhausted and he dearly wanted to sleep, he stepped into his office and checked the security cameras. Everything was cloud-based, and if need be, he could scroll through all of the video and still images that had been taken. But there hadn't been any activity during his trek.

Finally, he decided to check his email.

There were a dozen messages which he either read or immediately deleted.

The last one was curious.

It was from another mercenary he'd worked with in Europe years ago, and there was an attached image.

Tallon hesitated.

He knew computer viruses were often transmitted via attachments, but he also recognized the sender in this case, which gave him some measure of confidence he wasn't about to open an infected file that would ruin his network. Plus, his software was loaded with special security measures that would block any malware.

Tallon clicked on the image.

A face filled his computer screen.

At first, he couldn't place it.

But then the name linked cognitively with the pretty face staring back at him.

Jessica Halbert.

CHAPTER FIVE

Morning in New York meant a full-contact walk to the office. It was only a few blocks from her condo, but Lauren Pauling loved the time outside. In fact, she often walked home for lunch just to get out of the filtered air.

She stopped at the café next to her office building and bought a small coffee. No cream, no sugar. The barista, a young man with dark curly hair and expressive brown eyes, tried to flirt with her. She was flattered, but had a lot on her mind. Namely, the incredible size of the offer that had been made to buy her firm. She still couldn't believe it, but for now, she pushed it from her mind. It wouldn't do to be distracted from her current workload just because she was considering selling out.

She flinched at the term. Selling out. Was that what she was doing? Selling out? Technically, she was simply considering an offer. But exactly who would she be selling out? Her employees would continue on their current roles.

No, if she accepted the offer – and that was a big if – there would be no guilt. She had built the business by herself.

So if it was her decision to sell, she only had to answer to herself.

Pauling entered her own private office which consisted of a casual sitting area out front, and a separate private space in the back that housed her desk, computer, and guest chairs.

When she entered her private space, her eyes were immediately drawn to the thick envelope on her desk.

It was rare to receive a package this early in the morning. Ordinarily, FedEx didn't make its first delivery of the day until mid-morning which meant this was either an international delivery by a different courier, or that it had been hand-delivered.

The second thing Pauling noted regarding the package was its thickness. This was a serious collection of material. Either a thick book or two was encased in the packaging, or an extremely dense file. These weren't totally out of the ordinary. She often received substantial case files from existing or potential clients.

Pauling set down her briefcase on the desk, and took a drink from the cup of coffee. It was thick and rich, just the way she liked it.

Pauling sat down and took a closer look at the package.

The address label showed Pauling's investigative firm's location, with an address in Virginia on the return label.

She used a letter opener to cut through the thick layers of tape.

The envelope opened and Pauling slowly withdrew a set of thick folders, all held together by two thick, industrial-grade rubber bands.

The top folder had a square label and in its center were a series of bold, block letters.

Property of U.S. Army.

Pauling's brow furrowed. The army? Why in the hell would the army be sending her something?

She took a deep breath and opened the folder.

The first word in red leapt out at her.

Homicide.

Her eyes scanned the first document, looking for anything to do with her.

And then, at the bottom, she saw a name listed as the investigating officer.

Reacher.

CHAPTER SIX

The driver of the counterfeit hospital van heard the screams.

They were terror incarnate and all around him. The pleas for help were raw and ragged, coming from deep within the souls of humans consumed with extreme pain.

The smell of burned flesh added a texture to the horror, as did the sound of laughter and shouted commands.

In the distance, someone was playing American rock 'n roll from a tiny boom box that had probably been made in the 1980s.

People ran to and from. There was the sound of a vehicle starting its engine, the squawk of a handheld radio, in the distance, gunfire.

Madness.

Complete and total chaos had descended into a public hell.

It took a minute to realize the screams were his own. He was crying and begging, pleading for his life. They were the shouts and cries of a madman.

More importantly, they were ignored.

His body was on fire. Both literally and figuratively. The odor of charred flesh clogged his nostrils and he thrashed wildly against his captors.

They responded by stabbing him. His blood was being splashed across his own face. He could taste droplets in his mouth. Someone had smashed him in the face repeatedly with a crowbar and most of his teeth were gone. He had bitten down on his tongue and it too was bleeding. Blood poured from his mouth.

Through the slits of his swollen eyes, he could see the knives.

They reflected the flames of the fire that had been built in the center of the village. He'd lost track of how many blades there were. He simply knew that they were all different. A few short knives, a rusty machete, a bayonet that looked like it had possibly been used in the Second World War. It looked like whatever knife was handy, they had grabbed.

There was a woman wielding a butcher's knife going for his groin.

They were stabbing him but they weren't trying to kill him.

Not yet.

In fact, every time they cut him, they used a rod of super-heated and repurposed rebar to cauterize the wound.

They wanted him to live.

So he could suffer as long as possible.

His eyes were clenched shut but then suddenly, the music stopped. The sound of running footsteps ceased.

He opened his eyes as best he could.

A man stood before him with a wicked, curved blade. Razor-sharp, it gleamed in the orange glow of the fire.

The man's face was scarred and his teeth were missing.

He felt someone grab his hair to stretch out his neck and

then the man with the curved blade placed it against his throat.

He closed his eyes.

And opened them again.

He saw the ceiling of the cheap motel room, smelled and felt the cloying sweetness of the sweat that covered his body, brought on by the same nightmare that had haunted him all these years.

After a few minutes, the trembling stopped. The smell of his own burning flesh and leaking blood dissipated, leaving him cold and exhausted.

But focused.

It always had that effect on him.

In the nightmare, he was helpless.

Awake, he was motivated by a single, clear vision.

Revenge.

CHAPTER SEVEN

Tallon poured himself a cup of coffee. He'd had some of the best sleep of his life. Walking for 48 hours straight tended to induce quality shut-eye. But now he was awake, and the smell of coffee had never seemed better to him.

From his kitchen window, he saw the early morning sun creeping over the foothills that marked the beginning of Death Valley. He was reminded again of his choice to make this place his home. There had been some other considerations, namely parts of Montana and Idaho, but after touring the land there extensively, he decided against it. Tallon had also visited the Upper Peninsula of Michigan, a spot he'd been to previously, but also chose not to set up shop there. Mainly because of the long winters.

Tallon preferred the heat over the cold.

Which made his corner of the world perfect.

While some might consider his choice of living near Death Valley an odd one, knowing his past, Tallon viewed it as life-affirming. The barren landscape, harsh conditions and vast empty spaces were an illusion; in reality the land was full of living creatures and Tallon was inspired by the powerful life forces he saw on display every day.

There was nothing like fighting for one's life to be reminded just how precious it could be.

Now he took his coffee and sat in the leather club chair in his living room. It was his favorite room in the small home he'd acquired years before. It was a classic California adobe ranch, with white stucco walls and a Spanish tile roof. He'd practically gutted the interior of the place, fortifying it for security and adding some special storage rooms for guns and other equipment.

But the living room was where he spent the most time, other than his home office. The room was large, with a spectacular stone fireplace, a mid-century Native American rug covering the floor, and original artwork, mostly oil paintings done by local artists.

Against the backdrop of rustic ambiance, Tallon studied the smartphone in his hand.

His mind went back to the email he'd received just when he'd returned from his two-day hike.

The beautiful face of Jessica Halbert had looked back at Tallon.

Of course he'd remembered her. How could he not? She was a stunner. One of the most naturally beautiful women he'd ever encountered. All of her good looks were genetic as opposed to being manufactured by heavy doses of cosmetics and skimpy clothing. Being in the army, she rarely wore makeup and the natural curves of her body were often concealed by dull green pants and baggy shirts.

None of that mattered. She still turned heads wherever she went.

Part of it was because she had the kind of looks that stopped men in their tracks, but it was also because she'd radiated a warmth and honesty that was rare. It wasn't quite charisma, although she had a bit of that, too. It was more the recognition that when one met Jessica Halbert, they were meeting a good human being. Plain and simple.

He had known her only briefly, years ago. They had worked on a joint mission – overseen by a shadowy task force no one involved was allowed to understand. It might have been any of the collective alphabet groups: CIA, NSA, DEA, SpecialOps. Who knew?

Tallon had been one of the main players, Halbert had been support staff. After the successful completion of the mission, Tallon had made sure to bump into Halbert at the post-op drinking session, held in a local tavern near the army base from which the mission had originated.

They'd had a little fling that lasted no more than a couple of days. The sex had been wonderful, but both knew that's all it would be. Tallon wasn't stationed at the base, Halbert was. Their lovemaking had been intense, genuine, and full of caring. They'd even made vague plans to see each other again when Halbert had some R & R.

But it had never happened.

Tallon set down his coffee cup and swiped his smartphone to open the home screen. He launched his mobile browser and typed Jessica Halbert's name into the search window. He hit the return button and waited.

It took a few moments, but the first search results from the web began to populate his screen.

It didn't take long for Tallon to understand what had happened to her.

He set down his coffee and stared hard at his phone.

She'd been murdered.

CHAPTER EIGHT

D ue to death, retirement, and a shrinking pool of candidates eligible to meet the absolutely highest level of security clearances, their number was now down to three.

Three men.

Two white.

One black.

All of them were well past the point most call middle-aged. While none of them had begun to acquire additional padding around their waistlines, the three did share the development of the first vestiges of gray hair.

They weren't exactly humorless, in fact, the de facto leader of the group, the black guy whose name was Edgar, had been known in the past among the men under his command for his sharp wit and keen ability at satire. He could even do a fair impression or two.

No, the situation had long ceased to be one in which mirth and light-heartedness were welcome.

As both a group and individuals, the three men shared careers exemplified by staggering levels of success. Equally impressive was the fact that their portfolios of excellence were devoid of a single blemish.

They were working very hard to keep it that way.

The lone potential failure was the one they all shared and the reason for them meeting.

Along with Edgar, there was Jacobs, a hawk of a man whose face consisted of sharp angles, and nearly colorless light blue eyes. His body was devoid of fat, instead, his arms, neck and forehead were corded with thick veins.

The other man, Silvestri, was thick, dark and hairy. Known for his immense physical strength, he also possessed an animal cunning that had allowed him to survive scrapes that had taken the lives of many men not his equal.

"He's dead," Edgar said. "I'm sure of it." His voice was a deep and rich baritone, he could adjust for maximum impact. It was a tool he had used often to aid his command.

"We all know you can't be sure without a body," Silvestri said. "We've made that mistake before."

The electronic clock on the wall ticked once and the minute hand clunked onto the next mark. The sound echoed around the small room.

They were sitting in a conference room. It was only one of two spaces in the office that bore the name G & E Diversified Holdings, Inc. The name meant nothing. Some faceless minion in the vast government industrial complex had selected it, most likely from a list. Or maybe a bureaucrat figured having GE in the name would lend some sort of credibility.

It mattered little to the three men in the room.

They'd arrived separately, all of them driving dark SUVs with tinted, bulletproof windows.

The office itself consisted of a front door that only opened after biometric tests were passed. This included palm and retinal scans, as well as voice verification. There was an empty foyer where ordinarily a receptionist would sit, and the short hallway lead to the only space within which was now occupied by the three military men.

There was no rear entrance and the security system was military-grade.

"Agreed, but we can't wait for the body to turn up," Edgar pointed out. "We have to move forward based on some agreed-upon assumptions. My vote is to assume he's dead and act accordingly."

Jacobs rubbed his hatchet-like jaw. "He was a luxury. Someone to unwittingly perform the required footwork on our behalf. The entire time not knowing he was doing so. How are we going to replace him?"

"That's the big question," Edgar said. "The case was closed long ago. No one within the army is going to pick it back up unless we come up with an alternative solution."

"What about the package?" Silvestri asked.

"What package?" Jacob countered.

"The day before someone blew up his car with him in it," Silvestri lifted his chin toward Edgar. "Tell him."

"Surveillance recorded him going into a mall that included a mail drop," Edgar explained. "It's possible he sent something to someone. By the time we got inside, he was already on his way out. Footage showed he had something with him, but it was under his coat. On the way out, it looked like it was gone. He had very little time to do anything else. Not even buy a coffee or make a phone call."

"We've got people who can find out-"

"They're already working on it," Edgar cut off Jacobs. "We should know if he sent anything, and if he did, to whom it was sent. That information ought to be in our hands within twenty-four hours."

"What is our alternate plan?" Silvestri asked. "I don't like waiting. Waiting gets us nowhere."

"I figured you would say that," Edgar replied.

He pulled out a personnel file.

"Here's what I've initiated."

Silvestri and Jacobs glanced at the file and the face of the man looking back up at them.

Michael Tallon.

CHAPTER NINE

P auling's instincts were in full overdrive and all of them were throwing up red flags left and right.

She had no business being in possession of a classified army file, detailing what appeared to be a homicide case that bore the name of Jack Reacher. Pauling was fairly certain that it was illegal for her to even have the document.

It looked like a copy and not an original file, which made her feel a little better. She figured being in possession of an original government document was worse than a copy. Still, even copies of classified material were usually illegal to distribute, but she was no expert in that regard.

Nonetheless, she felt uncomfortable with the material staring back up at her. It shouldn't be here, and she shouldn't have it.

Yet, here it was.

Pauling sat back in her chair and sipped from her cup of coffee. She had a few options. She could tape the file back up and tell her secretary to send it back to the return address. Pauling could then claim that she hadn't opened it and had simply returned it promptly.

Or, she could make a copy and send back the original copy she'd received. That would at least allow her to read it at her own speed.

The other things she could do was simply dive in and start reading to see if it wasn't even worth the mental agitation.

Or she could toss the whole thing into the recycling bin and claim she'd never received anything.

Pauling knew she wasn't about to destroy the documents, which could potentially create a whole new host of problems.

Instead, the right decision was to send it back to where it came from. She also instantly recognized the ability to compromise. Read the file, see what it's about, and then send it back. She revisited the idea to make a copy of the copy, but that would put her on the same shaky ground.

She sent a note to her secretary to clear her schedule for the morning and then Pauling grabbed a fresh legal pad and pen, set it next to the package, and opened the file on top.

It was, indeed, a homicide report.

The victim was named Jessica Halbert, and she was a member of the army stationed on a base in Turkey. Her record showed no criminal misconduct. In fact, just the opposite. She'd been a success in all of her postings and had clearly been earmarked for greater things.

Pauling followed the narrative. Halbert had last been seen drinking at a local bar, left by herself, and then her body was later discovered in a forest nearby. She'd been raped and mutilated.

The suspect list was short. A few past boyfriends. Other people at the bar. Her personal items had been gone through, including her computer, email and social media accounts.

There had been no threats against her. No jealous ex-boyfriends. No sign of anyone wishing her harm.

Her cell phone had been the source of much time and effort among the investigators.

Reacher? Pauling wondered.

There had been nothing suspicious, save for a text message that had eventually been traced to a burner cell phone that was never used again. The message had provided next to nothing. It had simply been an agreement to meet outside the bar where Halbert was last seen.

The phone had certainly been destroyed, Pauling figured. And it had most likely belonged to the murderer. Which meant the killing had been premeditated, and not an act of passion.

She looked at the crime scene photographs and was glad she had skipped breakfast. They were as gruesome as one could imagine. Halbert's official army photograph was part of the file and Pauling saw that she had been a strikingly beautiful woman.

In no way reflected by the shocking brutality of the crime scene photographs.

Pauling took a quick glance at the rest of the files. They were mostly interview reports and witness statements.

She would read them later.

No, what mattered to her now was Reacher.

Had this been his case?

Pauling studied the return address, fired up her computer, and entered it into Google maps.

It pulled up the address of a veterans military hospital in Virginia. Was Reacher a patient there? Had he been injured and sent her this file as a way of asking her to investigate the case?

If so, why not call?

Or, more his style, why not just show up? He knew where she lived and worked.

Pauling saw there was a phone number along with the hospital's information, so she used her cell phone to call.

When the operator answered, she asked to speak to a

patient named Jack Reacher.

After a few moments, the woman responded, "We have no patient here under that name. Might he be under a different one?"

Pauling remembered that Reacher used to check into hotels using the names of former Yankees baseball players. It was the kind of thing she knew he did to amuse himself.

Well, there was no way she could guess the name that way.

Instead, she thanked the operator, hung up and considered her options.

Pauling had a lot on her mind. There was still the ridiculous amount of money she'd been offered for her firm.

There was a fairly large caseload she was overseeing, most of it being done by investigators on her staff. Still, the management took time.

Could she really afford to do what she was thinking of doing?

She got to her feet and stretched, took some deep breaths, and crossed the room to look out the window. The scene below was as busy as always. People rushing back and forth, trying to make a buck. Survival of the fittest and often the fastest.

Her mind went to Jessica Halbert. What had Pauling told herself last night about her DNA? That chasing bad guys was in her blood?

She returned to her desk, called her secretary and told her to postpone her meetings for the next two days and book her a flight to Virginia.

Pauling would go to the hospital and look for Reacher, or whomever sent the file.

Reacher could change his name, but he couldn't really change his appearance.

You could spot him a mile away.

CHAPTER TEN

A lcohol. Sweet nectar to the minds of military men and women. Booze was as integral a part of the life of a soldier as saluting, chow and regulations.

No matter where the Army, Navy, Marines or Air Force went, sales of booze shot up.

It was a great thing for him. He knew all about it. Knew the lifestyle. He even knew the favored bars of groups within the military.

Like the one he was focusing on tonight.

A group within a group.

A small, select team compromised of only a few members and tonight, he was focusing on one.

Why?

After he'd taken care of the patient in the hospital and dumped his body in the swamp, and after a sleepless night filled with nightmares of torture and suffering, he'd regained his focus.

And tonight, his focus was on one with whom he shared a history that needed to be rectified. Plus, the soldier in question had a delightful young girlfriend.

She was a real beauty. He'd done his requisite surveillance and despite his best intentions had fantasized immediately about what he could do to her.

Her name was Dawn. Red hair, cut stylishly short. Pale skin as smooth as ivory. All delicious curves on full display thanks to yoga shorts that practically made her amazing ass and inviting butt crack perfectly visible. The half T-shirt she wore exposed a flat stomach and tiny waist.

Dawn was what men called a "spinner." As in, get her in bed, sit her on top of you and spin away.

He watched Dawn and his target, a real blockhead named Doug Franzen, go into a bar called The Swing. Loud country music emanated from the place and there were vehicles parked everywhere, many of them four-wheel drive trucks and crotch rocket motorcycles.

The air smelled of beer, cigarettes and body odor.

This was a challenging situation for him. Not one he was afraid of, though. In fact, he took an incredible amount of pleasure from meeting the challenges of an operation like this.

Most of the important work had been done with makeup in his cheap motel room, putting on his "game face."

He parked his nondescript sedan quite far from the entrance to the bar, noting the location of Franzen's truck. He would need it later.

He crossed the parking lot and made his way inside the bar, ordering a beer from a female bartender wearing a straw cowboy hat and a thick flannel shirt. She was sweating profusely. Perhaps she was the source of the body odor smell.

Inside, the crowd was swelling. There was already very little room to maneuver and some of the things he'd used to blend into the crowd were already making him uncomfortable. He would have to move quickly while simultaneously conveying an air of perfect casualness.

Eventually, he made his way to where Franzen and Dawn were drinking. They had just returned from the dance floor and Franzen had chugged a huge pitcher of beer, with Dawn hooting by his side.

A waitress delivered more drinks to them and he sidled up next to Franzen.

"Don't I know you?" he asked Franzen. He mentioned the name of a military outfit he knew Franzen had been a part of.

"Oh yeah, sure!" Franzen said drunkenly. He clearly didn't recognize him, which was fine.

He grabbed the arm of the waitress and asked for shots of tequila.

He winked at Dawn, then dropped the names of some of the other men in the outfit. Franzen nodded along, clearly in the middle stages of intoxication.

When the waitress brought the drinks, he slid the vial of clear liquid from his pocket and into the palm of his hand. He, Franzen and Dawn tossed back the shots of tequila, but he threw his over his shoulder.

Dawn hooted again like a mentally challenged owl and she and Franzen engaged in a long deep kiss, during which he was able to pour the contents of the vial into Franzen's beer.

He raised his own beer and proposed a toast. "To the buddies who didn't make it back," he said.

Franzen raised his beer and together, they chugged the contents of their respective bottles.

He turned away, as if he had other people to talk to, and Franzen did the same, probably embarrassed that he couldn't remember the name of the buddy who'd just bought him some tequila.

It took a few minutes, but he saw in his peripheral vision Franzen stagger, and Dawn caught him before he fell.

He rushed over.

"Here, let me help," he said.

"I don't understand, Doug can drink anyone under the table."

"Maybe he just needs some fresh air."

Together, he and Dawn got Doug outside, which was no easy feat as they maneuvered the nearly comatose man through the crowded bar.

"Lower the tailgate on his truck, we'll sit there until he comes around," he told her, trying not to laugh.

Having her prepare the truck for him was highly enjoyable irony.

As he watched her incredible ass walk away from him, he turned to face Franzen.

"She's a real hottie, Doug. It's a shame you're going to kill her tonight."

CHAPTER ELEVEN

Tallon was perplexed.

He knew how incredibly difficult it was to trace anonymous emails. They could be sent from public IP addresses, routed through generic hosting accounts and automatically forwarded or deleted remotely.

Still, it bothered him.

Who had sent him a photo of Jessica Halbert, and why?

The obvious answer was that someone wanted him to discover that she'd been murdered. But what good would that do?

He'd certainly had nothing to do with her killing. According to the news reports he'd read, he wasn't even in Turkey at the time of her killing. His passport would prove that, among other things.

Certainly, he'd never been contacted by anyone regarding her death, so he must not have been on the list of suspects. Nowhere had he seen a mention that the case had been solved, so it would either still be an active investigation, or filed as a cold case.

He booted up his computer and looked at the email again. There was no message, no subject, and the email address was a collection of letters and numbers that appeared to be a jumble, randomly chosen.

After some debate, he forwarded the email to a technology-savvy friend and asked if there was anything he could find out for him.

Tallon figured the answer would be no, but he had to try.

Once he'd fired off the message to his geek buddy, Tallon let his mind drift back to the mission in Turkey where he'd met Jessica Halbert. Like just about every operation he'd ever been a part of, things hadn't gone as planned, yet the objective had been achieved. There'd been casualties, he remembered that.

Because the operation had been highly classified, there'd been no news reports of any kind. Additionally, the team had been relatively small in size and the scope equally modest.

Knowing full well that a "normal" day of work for him was unlike anyone else's. Still, he remembered quite clearly how everything had happened.

A terrorist cell had been identified, hiding in a small village across the border from Turkey in Syria. They'd done a smash and grab, lost one member of the team in the firefight, and been forced to leave one behind.

Afterward, they'd delivered the terrorist to a debriefing team and unloaded all of the information they'd been able to grab, including some computers and cell phones.

Back in Turkey, the team had celebrated with a few days off that included drinking, and for Tallon, a few nights with Jessica Halbert.

A few days later, he'd left Turkey and had never been back.

He really hadn't thought about her since then.

Until now.

When someone had anonymously emailed him a photo of her.

Tallon wondered if it was an innocent mistake.

Deep down, he figured it wasn't.

CHAPTER TWELVE

They met again in the office of G & E Diversified Holdings, Inc. It was rare for the three men to meet as a group, in person, two days in a row. But these were important times.

And Edgar had news.

"Lauren Pauling."

"Who the hell is Lauren Pauling?" Silvestri asked.

"She's a former FBI agent turned private investigator," Edgar explained. "She has a private firm in New York and does a lot of work for corporate, private and individual security. Only a few regular employees but she also employs a lot of specialist contractors. We also found out that she is currently sitting on a huge offer from one of her competitors."

"What did he send her?" Jacobs asked.

Silvestri consulted his notes. "That was my responsibility. Found out that she received a package that weighed just under three pounds."

"Files," Jacobs replied.

"Indeed."

"Maybe she can take his place," Silvestri said. "I know it's the obvious solution, but it's also one that requires no effort or involvement on our part."

"That's what I'm thinking," Edgar replied. "She might even be an improvement. And best of all, we remain hands-off."

"For now," Jacobs added. "I found out a little bit more about the car bomb that took out our friend. It was a device that had actually been stolen from a military warehouse here in the States. From my discussion with the commanding officer there, it was the only thing taken."

"Great," Silvestri said. "Untraceable."

The three sat in silence for a moment.

"You know, we're not really hands-off. Remember Michael Tallon," Silvestri pointed out. "We already got that ball rolling. And now we don't need him. This is why patience is so goddamned important."

"Maybe yes, maybe no," Edgar said. "He has a history with Pauling, which works in our favor. The two of them could make a formidable team."

"Tallon makes me nervous," Jacobs said. "I did some intel work on him beyond what we already know. Impressive. Not to be taken lightly."

A second uneasy silence fell between them. The office was empty, the only sound the occasional ticking of the wall clock, or a buzz from one of their cell phones. Edgar's phone did just that, putting an end to the quiet.

He picked up the phone and glanced at the screen.

"Okay, then," he said. He turned to show the image on display to Silvestri and Jacobs.

It showed a woman closer to fifty than forty. Quite pretty, with light-colored hair and a serious expression. It appeared to be the security camera facing the entrance to a hospital.

"That's Pauling?" Silvestri asked.

"Yes. She's at the hospital."

"She works fast."

Edgar nodded.

"Let's hope she's good, too."

CHAPTER THIRTEEN

L uckily, there had been an earlier morning flight out of LaGuardia, which allowed Pauling to fly to Virginia, rent a car, and drive to the hospital that sat just outside the small city of Norfolk.

It was an overcast day with a chill in the air, and the hospital did nothing to add cheer to the gloom. It was the worst kind of government architecture: a concrete box that looked more like a prison than a place of healing.

Pauling parked her car and entered the hospital, glad she had made it there before noon when people would start taking their lunch break.

After providing a photo ID and getting her photo taken, she was given a day pass which was a label with her name and photo. She stuck it on the front of her shirt, hoping it wouldn't ruin her blouse when she tore it off.

As much as she admired the men and women who worked as physicians and nurses, Pauling wasn't a big fan of hospitals. She'd been in many of them over her career as an FBI agent. Still, she knew the people who really ran a hospital were the charge nurses. They usually oversaw a team of a dozen or so nurses, sometimes divided by room numbers or floors. They tended to know exactly what was going on with everyone at any given moment.

Pauling started on the first floor. The charge nurse was named Angela, and she was short, with her black hair pinned back in a bun, and the woman wore a no-nonsense expression.

"I'm looking for a patient who may have been here recently," Pauling explained. "His name is Jack Reacher. Currently, you're not showing him as a patient, but sometimes, because of his line of work, he doesn't always use that name."

The nurse looked at her strangely, but as a military hospital, this kind of thing did occasionally happen.

"Are you family?" the nurse asked, glancing at Pauling's ID.

"I'm the closest thing he has to family, yes," she said. A bit presumptuous, but she needed the nurse's help.

"Well, how can I help you find him if you don't know the name he might be using?"

Pauling smiled. "He's a very distinctive man. At least 6' 5" with huge shoulders and arms. Sometimes people tease him and call him Bigfoot or Sasquatch. He wears his hair short, light sandy brown. He's been through a lot, has some scars and even a bullet wound or two."

Angela cocked her head and thought for a moment, but then slowly turned to a head shake indicating the negative. "Sorry, I don't have any patients who fit that description. You'll have to check with each charge nurse. We do it by the floor here."

Pauling nodded. That had been her plan.

She repeated the same procedure on the second floor with no luck.

On the third floor, she got an answer.

"Oh yes, the mystery man!" the charge nurse said. Her name was Cathy. She was tall, with thick glasses and a welcoming smile.

"So he was here?" Pauling asked, unable to keep the eagerness from her voice.

"Definitely. As soon as you talked about the shoulders, I knew who you meant."

"So what name is he registered under and what's his room number?" Pauling felt the drumbeat of excitement in her chest. She was excited to see Reacher again.

"Oh, he's not here anymore. He disappeared."

Pauling felt her hopes die within her.

"Disappeared? That's why you called him the mystery man?"

"Yeah, it was the strangest thing," Cathy explained. "He had been in a pretty bad accident. Had some surgeries to stop internal bleeding, and then he was gone. No one saw him leave. According to the hospital records, he never left. But his room was empty."

Pauling hung her head in frustration.

Now what, she wondered.

CHAPTER FOURTEEN

The wonderful thing about incredibly pale, alabaster skin was the shocking contrast it made when sliced open, revealing the blood-red meat inside.

He took his time with Dawn.

Even though he chose his victims carefully, she was special. Even better than Jessica Halbert, although that wasn't an accurate comparison.

He imagined Dawn could have been a supermodel, or a movie star, or if nothing else, the world's most highly paid porn star with a face and body like she had. He wondered again how the hell Doug Franzen had wound up with her. The guy's brain was as nimble as a sack of cement.

Dawn really had been an incredibly sexy young woman.

Emphasis on *had*, he thought, and chuckled.

Her face was now a mess, thanks to the frenzied beating he'd given her after he'd raped her repeatedly, finishing with a particularly vicious sodomizing.

He'd then performed surgery on the body most women would kill for. He smiled again both at the play on words and the idea that what he'd done with his knife could be considered surgical.

Yeah, only if the surgeon was out of his mind on Ecstasy or PCP and doing his most to inflict the greatest damage possible to Dawn's beautiful young body.

She had put up very little fight, thanks to a chloroform cloth he'd slapped over her mouth once they'd gotten Doug loaded onto the tailgate of his truck. The dosage for her was less than Doug's though. He wanted her semi-conscious for the sex, but not awake enough to fight him and risk leaving physical evidence like hair or DNA.

It had all gone very smoothly.

Once she was dead, he carefully arranged the scene, putting the knife in Doug's hands, making sure Doug's prints were all over the blade. He even used Dawn's fingernails to dig ragged furrows into the sides of Doug's face.

A lover's quarrel turned very violent.

How sad.

Two people with bright futures, maybe even a family down the road. Now it was all lost. Why couldn't people just get along and let the little things go?

If he was really lucky, Doug and Dawn might have had sex earlier in the day, before they'd decided to go out for a night of drinking and partying. Maybe when they'd gotten all gussied up for their night out, Doug couldn't help himself and had asked for a quickie.

If that turned out to be the case, Doug's DNA would be inside the victim. Along with plenty of his, that was for sure.

Perfect.

He'd chosen the scene of the crime carefully, allowing him the opportunity to leave Doug's truck with its crackerjack prizes inside and follow a footpath not visible from the road, back to his car.

Things were really coming together nicely. Doug had been

so drunk that he wouldn't remember the buddy who bought him a shot of tequila and their interaction had been so brief, witnesses wouldn't be able to recall them being together.

He'd been exactingly deliberate not to leave any evidence for law enforcement.

All in all, it had been an excellent night.

Now he would go to a new hotel and get some sleep, for once, looking forward to climbing into bed.

Whenever he killed, the sleep that followed was blissfully peaceful. No nightmares.

No memories of what he'd been put through.

He would awaken tomorrow morning with a smile on his face.

And focused on the next one.

CHAPTER FIFTEEN

"Yes, it's very unusual," the hospital's administrator told Pauling. Her name was Dr. Conrad, and she wore a white lab coat over a blouse with a muted floral pattern. She was well into her fifties with close-cropped silvery hair, and frameless eyeglasses. The eyes behind the lenses were alert and intelligent.

"At the same time, patients are under no obligation to remain with us," Conrad said. Pauling instantly knew that the matter of a patient disappearing had been discussed with the hospital's legal team and Dr. Conrad was speaking carefully along prepared lines.

Nothing scares a hospital more than a lawsuit, and losing track of a patient would certainly qualify.

"In fact, patients check themselves out of our facility more regularly than you might think," Dr. Conrad continued. "As a military hospital, we often have patients who are aggressive and not afraid to take matters into their own hands, including their own healthcare. It's a constant challenge but one we've learned to handle quite well over the years."

Except for the patient you just lost, Pauling thought.

"Was there an investigation?" she asked.

Dr. Conrad pondered the question for a moment. "No, I would say there was simply a confirmation the patient had left. A new bed had opened up, and we put it to use right away."

"Was the patient's name Jack Reacher?" Pauling asked. She was hoping the direct approach would work best.

"It would be a violation of hospital policy to divulge the names of our patients. All I can tell you is that we have not had a patient with that name, nor do we have one now."

Pauling decided to let the matter rest. She thanked Dr. Conrad, walked down to the main entrance, through the doors and out to her car.

She peeled off her temporary ID – it didn't ruin her blouse – and dropped it into the cupholder.

Dead end, she thought.

Pauling knew it would take a warrant to gain access to any kind of security footage the hospital had. That would require a police report, which would mean proof would have to be provided that a crime had been committed. And according to the hospital, there hadn't been.

A patient had left under his own power.

It happens, according to the hospital's chief administrator.

Unless family members came forward and claimed their loved one had been abducted, the mysterious sender of the package was gone.

Yet a man fitting Reacher's physical description had been a patient. And someone using Jack Reacher's name mailed her a package from the hospital.

It didn't take long for Pauling to realize that her options were limited. She put the car in gear, drove back to the airport and caught a flight back to New York. When the plane landed, she used an Uber ride to get her back to her condo.

By the time she had showered, changed into pajamas and climbed into bed, she was sure of two things.

One, someone, somewhere, desperately wanted her to investigate the murder of Jessica Halbert. Maybe it was Reacher, maybe it wasn't. Maybe someone had discovered the file, saw Reacher's name and learned of her past with him.

In any event, the file was there.

She had to decide if it was a case she thought worth pursuing. It would obviously have to be pro bono. There was no paying client here.

There was no client, period.

It was just the kind of thing she could technically afford to do if she sold her firm to her competitor. She would be set for life and could work cases that were all pro bono if she wanted to.

Pauling decided to get up early, brew a strong pot of coffee and read the file from front to back and then make her decision.

There was one more thing she was sure of.

She'd felt it at the hospital, on the drive back to the airport, and in the Uber on the way home.

At first, it had felt like paranoia.

But from the back of her Uber, using the camera on her phone to look behind her without turning her head, she had seen the big black SUV.

Someone was following her.

CHAPTER SIXTEEN

Every man or woman who has killed for their country must at some point face the moral dilemma within.

Are they a killer?

Do they enjoy taking the lives of others, even though it is in the service of a greater good?

When Doug Franzen stirred, forced his eyes open, and beheld the horror around him, he instantly knew the answer. He was sprawled in the front seat of his truck, and what was left of Dawn lay next to him. She was clearly dead, her nude body chopped and sliced into pieces.

His mouth was dry and he immediately vomited all over himself and the front seat of the truck. He pressed himself backward against the door.

His mind was screaming in panic.

He stumbled from the truck and wept on the ground. He couldn't believe what he'd seen.

Franzen forced himself back to his feet. On your feet, soldier, he told himself. And glanced back inside the truck.

It wasn't a dream.

He'd done it.

He'd killed her.

Probably in a drunken rage even though he never, ever got violent when he drank.

Now he knew.

He was a killer, plain and simple. Maybe he'd always known.

Because yes, he had enjoyed shooting bad guys overseas. Each time he put a bullet into an enemy combatant, he had felt a solid sense of satisfaction and looked forward to the next one.

Now, as he studied the bits of lifeless corpse of the woman he loved, he knew he had crossed the line. Maybe it had been the booze. Maybe they'd fought. He looked in the rearview mirror of his truck and saw the scratches down the side of his face.

He screamed until the screams became sobs.

He instantly knew what had happened.

They must have argued. Maybe Dawn had flirted with someone at the bar and he'd gotten jealous in his drunken stupor. Maybe he'd accused her of cheating on him. Things had escalated and she'd scratched him. And the careful control he'd always had over his own instincts had disappeared.

He'd killed Dawn.

And she was pregnant.

Which meant he'd also killed his unborn child.

Doug Franzen knew what he had to do. He'd made a career out of killing bad guys on behalf of the US military, and now he was the bad guy.

From beneath the seat of his truck, he found his gun. It was a small-framed .45 he kept for safety.

It was always there and always loaded.

He placed the muzzle beneath his chin, pointed up toward his brain.

And pulled the trigger.

CHAPTER SEVENTEEN

Pauling began by shrugging off the idea that she'd been followed. It was possible, but she also considered that she'd spent the day traveling back and forth from Virginia, had been frustrated by the lack of success, and had maybe been overly stressed.

There were probably tens of thousands of big black SUVs in New York.

Setting that issue aside, she settled into the case file that had been sent to her. It took Pauling several hours to read through the remaining witness statements and status reports in the army's official Jessica Halbert murder file.

It was near the end of the last report when she received a shock.

She saw a name she recognized.

Michael Tallon.

It was included in a statement made by one of Halbert's friends to the effect that the deceased had mentioned being attracted to a man named Michael Tallon. The friend didn't know if it was anything more than that. She said Halbert hadn't been around much during that time, but the friend had no idea where she was or who she might be with.

The investigator had done his due diligence and learned that Tallon was not in the country at the time of the murder so he hadn't followed up. It was at that point Tallon's name was officially removed from the list of suspects.

Pauling glanced at the clock on her phone. It was still early, but she knew Tallon would be up. Still, she decided to wait and see what else she could learn before she talked to him.

The last piece of paper in the file was confirmation the army's investigative unit had officially declared the murder a cold case, and put it in a holding pattern pending the discovery of new evidence. Pauling thought the move was a bit premature. She knew the military had seen a lot of budget cuts and there had been some pretty serious downsizing; in fact, she believed Reacher had been one of those cutbacks. So maybe the army's investigative branch was understaffed and overworked. Maybe they had a shorter window to close a case before it went into the cold file.

Or, maybe someone had wanted it to go away.

The other thing that gave Pauling pause was a clear and deliberate attempt to redact the name of the investigator. Save for the mention of Reacher on the first page, everywhere else the name of the person conducting interviews, gathering evidence, and filing reports was missing.

Why?

Pauling was no expert on the inner workings of the army, but it didn't take long to track down the unit in charge of handling the Halbert murder case.

Eventually, she was able to find a phone number for the special investigative team within that unit and make the call.

A woman answered.

Pauling explained who she was and that she might have evidence regarding the Jessica Halbert murder case.

"Please hold," the woman said.

Eventually, a man picked up on the other end of the line. He spoke in a clipped, officious tone that conveyed he'd been interrupted.

"This is Watkins," he said. "With whom am I speaking?"

"I'm Lauren Pauling, former FBI agent working as a private investigator," she said. Pauling knew she had to tread carefully and avoid mentioning that she had a copy of their murder file. "I'd like to speak to the person handling the Halbert case."

"I'm handling the case," Watkins said, his tone altering slightly. "What can I do for you?"

"Oh," Pauling said. "I was told Jack Reacher was working the case."

"Reacher?" Watkins asked. "I've heard of him, but no. He's not involved. He left the army a long time ago, I believe."

Then why is his name on this file? Pauling wanted to ask, but knew she couldn't.

"How can I help you, ma'am?" Watkins broke in on her thoughts. "Do you have information pertaining to the case?"

Pauling made a decision to cut her losses.

"No, I was simply trying to get ahold of Jack Reacher for something else. I apologize for the intrusion."

"Yes ma'am," Watkins said and broke the connection. A bit quickly, Pauling observed.

She stared at her phone.

This is all wrong, she thought.

She set the file aside and went into her home office where she fired up her desktop computer.

Using the search terms of *Jessica Halbert*, *murder*, *army* and *investigation*, she read through the results.

It was a disappointing effort. There was virtually no information other than the original news articles reporting the murder.

What was interesting to Pauling, though, was what wasn't included.

Namely, there was no mention of anyone named Watkins. No mention of Reacher. And most telling of all, no contact information provided for civilians to come forward with evidence.

All of which was highly unusual.

Finally, frustrated, Pauling picked up the phone.

It was time to call Michael Tallon.

CHAPTER EIGHTEEN

"Sorry buddy, no can do."

Tallon listened to his friend's voice on the other end of the line. His name was Vogel and he'd spent some time investigating the email sent to Tallon containing Jessica Halbert's photo.

"I figured," Tallon responded. "It looked like it would be tough to trace."

"Yeah, that thing went straight into a rabbit's hole." Vogel was extremely talented at what he did and if he couldn't find the source of the email, then most likely no one could. "Anonymity is so easy these days, with private servers and public Wi-Fi. If you add in someone who actually knows what they're doing and how to mask certain maneuvers, it's virtually impossible."

"And that's what was done here?"

"Absolutely. That email came from behind a wall. But even worse, there's no way to know which wall. You get me?"

"Yeah, I do."

Vogel let out a breath, and Tallon knew he was smoking.

A bit of a rarity these days, but Tallon had never seen the man without a cigarette dangling from the corner of his mouth.

"The photo was interesting, though," Vogel offered.

Tallon's ears perked up. "How so?"

"Every piece of digital matter has code," Vogel explained. "Some visible. Some not. Even if you work to clear metadata from a file, there is always code because that's what digital entities are made of."

"So what did the code tell you?" Tallon asked. He knew Vogel had something and was trying to draw it out.

"That photo was not a publicly available file."

"You mean it was classified?"

"Not exactly." Tallon heard Vogel suck in some nicotine and then blow it back out. "That code had a very specific lineage that was never produced elsewhere. It was fairly simple to trace and determine that it could only have come from one location. Now, unfortunately, that location was behind a wall."

"Just like the email."

"Yep, but unlike the email and its address, at least I know which wall it is."

"And that would be?" Tallon was losing his patience.

"The US Army."

At first, Tallon was tempted to dismiss the information. Of course it was an army photo. Halbert was in the army.

But the more he thought about it, the more he realized what Vogel was saying.

"So what you're saying is that if the photo could only have come from within the army's network, the email was probably sent from someone with access to it."

"Mostly correct," Vogel hedged. "In my line of work, we never make absolute statements because as soon as you do, someone will work to create an exception."

"Hackers love challenges," Tallon said.

"It's what they live for. Back to the photo, though, I would caution you to not assume only army personnel have access to army records. I would expand your conclusion to include anyone in the government. Because I've been in their systems before and it's like a hoarder's living room. There are servers, firewalls, back doors, trap doors and everything in between....everywhere. Only the federal government could create such a mess."

Tallon was afraid of that. His search window now consisted of a group of people that numbered in the millions.

He thanked Vogel and disconnected. Tallon put his phone on the kitchen table and was about to start making himself breakfast when his security system alerted him to the presence of a vehicle entering his driveway.

That was odd, no one ever visited his home. For one thing, it was remote, and for the other, he had a post office box so not even the postal service delivered.

Tallon went to his office and looked at the security screen.

A big black SUV.

Two men were getting out.

They looked like they worked for the government.

And their hands were inside their jackets, clearly getting ready to draw their weapons.

CHAPTER NINETEEN

H e'd done a good amount of killing in just a day or two.

First, he'd euthanized the big guy in the hospital and dumped his body in the swamp.

And then he'd hacked beautiful Dawn into little pieces.

Now safe and sound in his new hotel room, he was watching the television with great enthusiasm.

The television reporter announced, "It appears to be a murder-suicide."

The man in the hotel room clapped his hands together and laughed. "You're exactly right," he said to the television screen and the reporter standing just outside the area where they'd found the butchered body of Dawn and Doug Franzen, the victim of a self-inflicted gunshot wound.

"It does *appear* to be a murder-suicide."

He snorted with laughter.

It was always like this. Riding high after a killing, and then he knew the road ahead was pointed downward with the potential of hitting a very dangerous low point if he didn't regain focus.

But now, he was on a high. Adrenaline. Mania. Whatever the psychologists might call it, he didn't care.

He'd had his fun and gotten to kill another one of *them*.

That's what mattered.

Along the way, he'd taken full advantage of the opportunity to do what he really enjoyed, too. All of his life he'd fantasized about tying up, raping and killing women. When he'd read about the real-life serial killer in Wichita who called himself BTK for Bind, Torture, Kill, he'd recognized a kindred spirit.

He got up off the bed and walked into the bathroom. He wore no shirt, and studied himself in the mirror.

It was an ugly sight.

His upper body was deformed with dozens of scars. There was scar tissue everywhere, and most of it was from burns. Great pink swatches of saggy, plastic-looking skin that resembled nothing human hung from his body like a crooked quilt.

His face bore the results of a severe beating. A jaw that didn't work correctly. An eye that had never healed and hung slightly at half-mast. He wore his hair slightly longer to hide the fact that one of his ears had been completely cut off.

The skin on his face? Well, that wouldn't win any beauty prizes, either.

He turned away from the mirror and walked back into the bedroom. Glancing down, he looked at his left foot, which was missing all of its toes. They'd been hacked off one by one.

It was a minor miracle that the mob had failed to cut off his genitals. He still remembered that local tribeswoman who'd looked eager to start the job with a big butcher's knife.

She was the one he most often saw in his nightmares.

Thankfully, he was still a man with all of the glorious body parts God had given him.

But he wasn't just a man.

He was a man beyond the law.

It was the role the universe had assigned him, he'd decided. That woman with the butcher knife had been stopped not by a drone strike or a bomb dropped by an American aircraft, it had been a miracle delivered directly from forces more powerful than man.

It wasn't God who'd sent it, he knew.

It was the devil.

His devil.

Saving him from death, giving him life. And with a life, came a quest for a life's work. He'd found his the first time he'd killed.

Soon, he realized he could combine his passion with his incredible thirst for revenge.

A win-win.

Or a kill-kill.

He smiled again.

This time, the rigid scar tissue on his face, which he disguised when he went out for a kill, turned the smile into something else.

Something not quite human.

CHAPTER TWENTY

F eeling negligent, Pauling left her condo and went to
the office.

There, she first tended to seemingly endless
details of running a company. She worked furiously for several
hours meeting with her subordinates, answering emails,
submitting invoices, and arranging her calendar.

Only when she was caught up with her firm's work did she
take a moment to consider the Jessica Halbert case.

She had to decide. Was she in, or was she out?

Pauling drummed her fingers on her desk. She thought
about Reacher but quickly realized this was not about him.
His name was what had drawn her into the case, and certainly
merited the trip to the veterans hospital. But now it was
about more than that.

It was about a cold case involving a murder.

And try as she might, she was struggling to separate it
from the offer to buy her firm. The obvious move was to sell
her company and make the Halbert case her first "personal"
investigation.

Still, she didn't have to work it that way.

Besides, the process of selling the company, submitting all of the paperwork to lawyers, and actually disentangling her role from the firm would take time. Plenty of time to work on the Halbert case, if she so chose.

Plus, the idea of selling an organization she had built from scratch outweighed the recent arrival of the mysterious file from a hospital patient who then promptly disappeared. It would be foolish to rush the decision on something that had literally just come across her desk.

Pauling wasn't sure how much time had passed when she leaned forward in her chair and tapped out a message to her assistant.

Clear my schedule for the next few days.

With one decision made, Pauling immediately went to her computer and launched her browser. With a few clicks of her mouse, she arrived at the portal to the FBI's database. It was a point of entry she should no longer have access to but with the help of a contractor she frequently employed, it was arranged for her credentials to remain intact while also leaving no breadcrumbs from her coming and going.

Once in, she worked her way through the system and managed to get into shared military files that included counterinsurgency operations in Turkey. Pauling narrowed the search to documents that matched the timeframe of Jessica Halbert's murder.

While the server processed her requests, she thought hard about what she should be looking for.

One, the primary investigator. He or she would have the essential details of the case and the suspects. She had the files, but it was the information *not* in them she needed. It was the kind of detail only available by talking to the primary detective in person.

Or at least, on the phone.

Once she had that name, she could see if there were any

updates on the suspects. Had any of them been cleared? Died? Come up with an alibi?

Finally, her screen blinked to life and she saw a subset of folders matching the criteria she had input. She clicked and dragged them onto her desktop, but still left the window to the FBI's server open.

Just in case she quickly learned something, she could go back in and do a second search. For insurance, though, she tended not to linger on the server. Pauling figured the more time she spent digging through the files, the greater her chance of being discovered.

She minimized the server window and clicked on the first of the files. She was disappointed to find hundreds of subfolders and files. There was a lot of information.

Pauling began to open them one by one, and soon discovered a pattern to the naming conventions of the files and was able to separate them by category. Eventually, she had separated the folders that pertained to criminal investigations within the army during the time of Jessica Halbert's murder.

It was a start and soon, she was working much faster and efficiently.

Eventually, she found what she was looking for.

The mystery patient had sent her a stack of copied files and although the top document had carried the name of Jack Reacher, the rest of them had been redacted.

Now she was looking at the original files and they showed no signs of Jack Reacher's name or involvement.

It quickly became apparent that the primary army special investigator was a man named Thomas Wainwright. Some of the documents were emails directed to "Tom" and other statements were signed with the initials "TW" or just "W."

Pauling opened up a new browser window and Googled the terms Thomas Wainwright and army investigator.

A series of articles appeared.

It seemed there was a meteorologist in Utah named Thomas Wainwright. As well as a 12-year-old chess prodigy with the same name.

Pauling clicked instead on an image search and halfway down the results page, she spotted him. It was a photo of a man wearing shorts and a T-shirt with the word Army across the front. He was smiling toward the camera, and holding a trophy of some sort.

And he was huge. Massive shoulders. Long arms thick with muscle, and a rugged, if not overly handsome face.

He looks like Reacher, Pauling thought.

A dead ringer, in fact.

Suddenly, Pauling knew beyond the shadow of a doubt that Thomas Wainwright was the man in the hospital. He was the one who had copied the file and sent it to her, signing his name as Reacher.

Why?

Had someone in the army known Reacher and pointed out to Wainwright that he looked just like him? Or had he found out about Pauling's past connection with Reacher and decided to reach out to her for help but instead of signing his own name he signed it as Reacher. Either to deceive Pauling, or to keep his name out of it.

If it was the latter, why?

She closed the image file and was about to close the search results when she found an article at the very bottom of the page.

It detailed an explosion near an army base that had been earmarked as a possible terrorist attack. There had been one victim critically injured who was fighting for his life in intensive care.

Thomas Wainwright.

It explained why he was in the hospital.

And it maybe even explained his need for secrecy.

The only thing it didn't explain: what exactly the whole thing had to do with her.

She glanced down at her phone.

Why hadn't Tallon responded yet?

What was he doing?

CHAPTER TWENTY-ONE

Having spent the better part of his adult life in the company of both military men and law enforcement, Tallon knew what he was seeing.

Or, more accurately, what he wasn't seeing.

In the case of the two men, he knew immediately they weren't military, and they certainly weren't cops.

In Tallon's line of work, small details often made the difference between life and death.

As he quickly took stock of the images on his security monitor, a few things immediately leapt out.

For starters, the black SUV was definitely not military-grade. It reeked of private contractor. Tallon could tell by the way the vehicle sat, and the quality of the tint in the windows that it certainly wasn't reinforced with armor and the windows were not bulletproof. This vehicle had been driven directly off a car dealer's lot.

The suits the men wore were clearly of a higher quality. Tallon could tell they were tailored, which made spotting their shoulder gun rigs all the easier. Another big tell – most in law enforcement had off-the-rack suits that were roomy enough to camouflage their weaponry. Real plainclothes cops made a habit of not advertising their hardware.

These two clearly didn't follow that protocol.

Not to mention, the kind of suits they were wearing required a budget well beyond typical law enforcement or standard government salaries.

This, too, spoke to private security.

Finally, the fact that they had already begun to draw their weapons was another clear sign of rogue actors. It spoke to being overly aggressive, as opposed to following standard procedure.

These guys were private, or at the very least, very poorly trained.

Tallon completed his threat assessment and immediately went into action. He already had a gun in hand and now he shrugged on a bulletproof vest, then pulled on a baggy T-shirt.

He went to the front door, and casually opened it.

"Morning," he said.

"Michael Tallon?" the one on Tallon's left said. He was a big guy, with pale, sweaty skin, blond hair cropped close, and black sunglasses. His voice was unusually high-pitched. Tallon wondered if he'd added so much bulk as compensation.

"No, he just stepped out. Something about a farmer's market downtown. Who's asking?"

The guy on Tallon's right didn't move.

He knew what they were thinking. They'd probably been given a photo of him and now they were trying to gauge if the man on the doorstep in a baggy t-shirt, messy hair and gym shorts was one and the same.

It could be a relative. A brother maybe.

Tallon knew they were both wondering how to proceed.

Double check the photo or photos they'd been given for reference? But that would imply they were less than confident and they had already drawn their guns. They were ready for action and the idea of withdrawing was not the path they wanted to take. It was tentative, and these guys were all about aggression and power.

The man on Tallon's right moved first. He was shorter than the blond but matched his partner in terms of width. A short, squat weightlifter, Tallon figured. He'd probably worked as a bouncer before trying to move up into private security. He clearly was not the leader, which is why he glanced over at the blond.

The blond man nodded his head forward almost imperceptibly and that's when Tallon knew they weren't going to verify they had the right man. Instead, both of them raised their weapons.

Tallon was already firing. He'd kept his gun low but had already raised the muzzle during the pair's moment of hesitation. In a situation like this, it didn't pay to be the one reacting.

He shot the blond first, a double tap that resulted in the back of the man's head being blown off in a shower of blood and brains. He toppled over backwards and his pistol fired harmlessly into the air.

Tallon dove to the side as bullets ripped into the door and he swung it shut, rolled to his side, and raced along the interior wall. He heard more popping sounds, and knew the man was firing into the windows, not realizing they were bulletproof glass.

Finally, Tallon reached the end of his interior hall, ducked through the back door, and came around the side of the house.

The advantage was all his and he used it to maximum effect. He guessed the man was racing toward the same corner, not realizing that the grounds were all under video surveillance. Tallon simply took cover behind the low stucco wall that tapered down from the corner of the house and took out his phone. He tapped an icon on the screen and he saw the feeds from his security cameras. He took a quick look at the frame in the lower right, which pointed back at the front of the house from the front of the property.

He saw the man was standing with his back to the wall, not yet moving around the corner of the house. He stood with his gun pointed at the corner of the property, waiting for Tallon to appear.

Instead, Tallon waited, too. He had his gun trained on the corner, but he kept one eye on the video stream. Tallon watched as the man's head bobbed in a rhythm and Tallon could only imagine him counting in his head, one, two, three...

The man pushed off from the wall.

Tallon let go of his phone, saw the man come into view around the corner and Tallon shot him twice in the face.

The man pitched forward, landing on his dark sunglasses, his feet twitching as the last vestiges of life poured from the bullet holes in his face onto the sandy soil of Tallon's yard.

He hadn't even gotten off a single shot.

The house was remote enough that Tallon had no need to worry about gunfire alerting his neighbors. Plus, the dead man in front of him couldn't be seen from the street.

It was the dead blond man in the driveway he had to take care of immediately.

As he raced forward, he realized that his instincts had been right.

The email with Jessica Halbert's photo?

It had only been the beginning.

CHAPTER TWENTY-TWO

As hardened as the three men were who collectively met under the banner of G & E Diversified Holdings, Inc., they nonetheless were disgusted with what they saw. On the table in the conference room were images of the crime scene from the Doug Franzen murder, and his girlfriend Dawn Fitzgerald.

"A goddamned animal," Edgar said. His dark face was a shade more sinister than usual as he pondered the images.

"He's getting worse," Silvestri said. "His disease is progressing. He's killing faster and faster, and more violently than ever. If that's possible."

Jacobs said nothing. The lean man uncoiled his greyhound-like body from the conference room chair and stood, pacing back and forth. "This simply can't go on. We've got to consider the option that none of us have wanted to discuss."

"No," Edgar said. "We have to stay the course. We've got Pauling working now, and she'll be joined by Tallon. Together, they make a much better team than Wainwright."

"Speaking of Wainwright, where the hell is he?" Silvestri said. "If he's dead, where's the body? He gets snatched from the hospital and then what? You'd think our friend would have put it on full display as a message to us."

"Maybe he wanted to keep us guessing," Edgar said.

"Well, I'm tired of this son of a bitch," Jacob said. The regularly bulging veins in his face and forehead were sticking out even more. They were throbbing as the blood was rushing to his face. "And I'm tired of us dicking around like this. Look at us! We're three of the most decorated soldiers and commanders the American military has ever seen. Yet here we are, sitting in this shithole office in a strip mall for chrissakes, carrying on like a bunch of nervous housewives. Screw the help. Screw the plans. Let's all three of us go out there and do what we should have done a long time ago. Take matters into our own hands and put a bullet in this sick dog once and for all."

Edgar and Silvestri said nothing. Jacob's words echoed throughout the room.

Finally, Edgar sighed and said, "Feel better?"

Jacobs glared at him.

"I'll offer a compromise," Edgar said at last. "Let's give Pauling and Tallon 48 hours. If they haven't found him, we activate the plan you mentioned, which, I might add, puts us at considerable risk of being exposed, and go after him ourselves."

"I'm sure Dawn Fitzgerald's family would say we waited a tad too long already," Jacobs added.

"Take it easy, Jacobs," Silvestri said. "Emotions have no place on the battlefield. And make no mistake, we're at war with this son of a bitch."

"Yeah," Jacobs said. "And he's winning."

CHAPTER TWENTY-THREE

Pauling left the office and walked to a French restaurant less than three blocks from her building.

She'd been poring over the Jessica Halbert case files and needed a break, some fresh air, and some nourishment. The restaurant was rarely crowded, a hole-in-the-wall really, but the food was excellent.

Pauling ordered a mixed salad and a cup of garbure, which was a thick soup made with vegetables and ham. She chose a bottled water to drink.

Her table was next to the window and while she waited for her food, she watched the pedestrians hurry by and thought about the Halbert case.

It was obvious, after she'd dug through the incredible amount of information she'd appropriated from the military's own files, that a severe amount of redacting had gone on. Not so much with regard to Jessica Halbert's murder, although there had been some pretty heavy editing there, too, but the operations she may or may not have been involved in.

Army stuff that qualified as beyond the ordinary daily grind that represents most of what goes on in a military base.

Specifically, censorship was employed on missions like the one that had included Tallon.

Pauling had found it in the files that concerned activities that took place several months before the murder. From what she could tell, Halbert was involved in nothing out of the ordinary, other than the mission that Tallon was a part of. Coincidence?

Pauling didn't believe in those. Part of what had attracted her to working for the FBI was her analytical personality. While she did believe that sometimes truth was stranger than fiction she also believed that chalking things up to fate was usually a mistake.

In this case, she considered being chosen as the recipient of the mystery files that also included a link to Michael Tallon was not mere happenstance.

There had to be a reason.

The waiter, a crisply dressed man with a pencil-thin mustache and perfect posture, brought Pauling her salad and soup along with a small basket of bread.

The soup smelled fantastic, but Pauling started with the salad. Everything about the restaurant's dishes spoke to fresh-ness. The lettuce and vegetables had a pleasant crunch and the right amount of tenderness.

As she ate, she continued to operate under the presump-tion that she was chosen for a reason. While admitting that it wasn't an absolute certainty, the obvious conclusion was that Tallon's mission which also involved Jessica Halbert might just have been the catalyst for her murder.

Or, if nothing else, the reason for Pauling receiving the case files.

Perhaps it was both.

Pauling knew Tallon frequently worked "off the books" for both the government and private companies. She also knew him as a man with honor and integrity. So Pauling also made the assumption that the military operation he and Halbert had taken part in was probably legitimate.

Up to a point.

Or at least a gray area between absolute right and wrong.

Yet the odds favored a connection.

Pauling glanced at her phone, saw there was still no word from Tallon.

She finished her lunch and wished she'd ordered the bowl of soup as opposed to the cup, but knew she'd feel she made the right choice when she was working out tonight.

Pauling left the restaurant but didn't go straight back to the office. Instead, she walked briskly in a roundabout way, occasionally using the reflections in store windows to see if anyone was following her.

She saw no one.

Back at the office, she dug into the files once again.

Pauling needed names.

The first problem was that any and all commanding officers' names for the mission were completely censored. Even the name of the operation was blacked out. The only way Pauling could track the exercise in question was by a series of numbers and letters representing a shorthand code for certain army "projects."

What she could deduce were the intermediate players, thanks to Michael Tallon. If his name was visible, then that meant he wasn't a commanding officer, but rather, an operative.

Which also meant the names associated with Tallon, and there were only three, were also operatives.

The names grouped with Halbert's were clearly support staff, like her. Pauling couldn't eliminate them from being involved, but for now, she would focus on the three names equal in rank to Tallon.

Peter Maitling.
Christopher Zenz.
Doug Franzen.

CHAPTER TWENTY-FOUR

Tallon found the keys to the black SUV still sitting in his driveway.

The keys were in the front pants pocket of the dead blond-haired man sprawled a few feet from the vehicle's front bumper. Tallon saw the button sporting the icon of the SUV's rear hatch door and he pressed it.

The door automatically began to rise.

Grabbing the dead man by the ankles, Tallon dragged him around to the rear of the vehicle. He gripped the dead man's belt and the front of his shirt, and dead lifted the corpse into the rear cargo area of the SUV. No easy feat, as the man easily weighed well over two hundred pounds.

Once Tallon had the body inside the vehicle, and clear from view, Tallon dug out the man's wallet and cell phone. He took a quick glance at the driver's license and noticed it was issued by the state of Maryland.

Interesting.

He slipped both the wallet and the phone into his own pockets and then he thumbed the key fob's button again to close the door.

Back around the end of the house, he heaved the second dead man over his shoulder, knowing that the blood would smear onto his own clothes but also understanding it couldn't be helped.

It was a dirty job, and he had to do it.

Tallon once again keyed the SUV's rear door open and dumped in the second body. Repeating the process, Tallon retrieved the second dead man's cell phone and wallet and added them to his pockets.

Next, he retrieved the dead men's guns from where they'd dropped them on the ground and carried them into the SUV as well. They were standard issue 9mm pistols, Brownings.

A good, dependable gun in the right hands.

Tallon left the guns loaded and dumped them into the big vehicle's glove compartment. He also took a quick look around the interior and saw two small suitcases as well as a laptop case.

It confirmed what he'd already known; these men weren't law enforcement. They were private security. Hired contract killers and not exactly the cream of the crop. Clearly, they hadn't been properly briefed on their target or maybe they'd just been overconfident. But relying on bluffing and a half-assed attempt to appear as cops was not a serious effort.

Tallon wondered why.

When things seemed too easy, it almost always meant difficulties would follow.

Well, Tallon would be prepared for that.

He went back into the house, collected the gear he knew he would need and that always stood ready for situations just like this. Most of it was already packed into a military-grade backpack which contained spare IDs, guns, ammunition, and five thousand dollars in cash. In the side pockets were an array of electronics, including at least two burner phones that hadn't been used but were fully charged.

A duffel bag was also packed and ready to go. It contained several days worth of clothes as well as the basics in toiletries.

He retrieved his own keys, wallet and cell phone. When he was prepared to leave, he carefully armed the home's extensive security system.

Back outside, he clambered into the black SUV, set his bags in the passenger seat and drove away from his home, heading directly west toward Los Angeles.

As he drove, he was careful not to exceed the speed limit, considering he had two murder victims in the back.

His mind wandered and led him to ponder the timing of the email containing Jessica Halbert's photo, his reading about her murder, his tech friend's message that the email came mostly from within a government entity, and now, the two dead men in the back of the SUV.

He glanced at his phone and saw that Lauren Pauling had called. Tallon debated about calling her back and decided against it for the time being. For one thing, he didn't want his cell phone to ping a tower at the moment, at least not until he disposed of the bodies.

The other reason was that when he did talk to her, he wanted to be able to focus on the conversation. It would be better to wait until he'd settled the matter at hand before he talked with her.

For the disposal job, he chose a place he'd scouted from time to time. Tallon knew Death Valley and the surrounding area better than anyone. He ran here all the time, often driving to a new location to explore on foot. It kept him sharp, but also provided opportunities like this.

In particular, he knew one side road on the southern end of the park that branched off into a little used track that was once a service road but had been abandoned years ago. The site was never visited by tourists, and it officially didn't exist on maps, even digital versions with GPS.

Now Tallon steered the SUV down the road, a cloud of dust behind him, and engaged the vehicle's four-wheel drive. The terrain was steep and rocky, graduating to little more than desert terrain with no discernible road at all.

Ahead, he saw the branch he was looking for and followed it several miles until a gulley appeared. He parked the SUV, unloaded the bodies, and rolled them down the embankment. The process was a twofer in that loose stones and gravel followed the bodies down and at least practically covered them.

Tallon then used his feet to help gravity along, and soon, both of the wannabe killers were covered by rock, dirt and dust. He felt no guilt at leaving the dead men in unmarked graves. They'd made the choice to go after him and now they were suffering the consequences.

Tallon went back to the SUV, turned it around and eventually reconnected to the road heading west.

According to his calculations he would be in Los Angeles in less than three hours. There, he would wipe down everything to avoid leaving prints, ditch the vehicle along with his bloody clothes and lay low.

And then he would call Pauling.

CHAPTER TWENTY-FIVE

There had been no nightmares.

But even in times of quiet and calm, he remembered what had happened in southern Turkey when he'd almost been murdered by a mob of crazed locals. Yes, he'd certainly played a role in their anger.

He could still see their enraged faces.

It was easy to transport himself back to that moment.

When all of those psychotic faces had been wiped away by a blinding flash that had penetrated his closed eyelids, it was like a sudden gust of hot steam blasting him in the face.

All at once, he knew it wasn't his tormenters inflicting a new kind of pain upon him. No, this was something else. Something bigger.

Something far more wicked.

He opened his eyes and saw that he wasn't the only thing on fire.

The whole world was being consumed with flames.

Since he had been at the center of a vicious mob, surrounded by a ring of people three layers deep, it was they who had absorbed the impact of the blast, sent from above.

Body parts were everywhere. The stench of gasoline, burnt flesh and chemical residue filled the air.

At his feet were a pile of charred body parts. A head, completely severed from its body, was tucked between his ankles. The blank eyes stared up at him.

Somewhere, someone screamed.

He wasn't the lone survivor, he realized.

It galvanized him into action. A chain around his left arm was now completely loose. He pulled on it, and a metal pole snagged on the bloodied torso to his left. He pushed the body away and the pole went with it, allowing the chain to slide free from his arm.

He staggered to his feet.

Blood gushed from his open wounds and parts of his body sagged under the weight of loose burnt flesh.

He knew he was alive, but barely.

He also knew that he had been abandoned.

And why.

It didn't matter. What he knew from the unit's reconnaissance is that there was a pickup truck at the rear of the compound, with a machine gun anchored in the truck bed.

He staggered across the minefield of body parts, passed through an empty tent and found the pickup truck. It was unlocked so he climbed inside and looked for the keys. They were on the floor.

His hands shook as he picked them up and found the right key. He turned the ignition and the engine roared to life. All around him, smoke billowed, and the roar of dozens of fires filled the air.

He drove away from the small village and no one saw him leave. No one tried to stop him and no one shot at him.

They were dead, most of them.

He had no idea where he was going.

All he knew was that for now, he couldn't go back.

But eventually, he would.

He thought of that now as he prepared to leave his cheap hotel room and go back out into the world.

There had been a message on his burner phone from the only person in the world who actually saw him for his true self. It was an interesting message with information that required swift and accurate attention.

He gathered his things, applied the various accessories required to camouflage his true self, and left the room.

When the sun hit his face, he was reminded of that moment when he'd left the smoldering village in the stolen truck.

And with the super heated sound of human suffering and the air tinged red with blood and fire, he remembered how he'd felt the first stirrings of a vengeance that would fuel him.

It wasn't a rebirth, he would realize.

It was resurrection.

CHAPTER TWENTY-SIX

Pauling was back in her office and pacing. She'd gotten out from behind her desk, sat on the couch in the small sitting area and read through the files again. Then she'd gotten up and started pacing.

Peter Maitling.

Christopher Zenz.

Doug Franzen.

The three names included in the files along with Michael Tallon. Three men who'd been on the last mission before Jessica Halbert's murder.

Pauling knew she had learned just about everything she could from the file and from the paperwork. It was time for some intelligence gathering of her own.

She went back to her desk, sat down at her computer and entered all three names into a separate software system she used that was a skip tracer's dream, thanks to its highly illegal access to private databases.

All three names came back with addresses. There were no redundancies because Pauling had included military service dates along with the search request.

These were the three men she needed to speak to, no question.

Linking the names and addresses to a database that utilized reverse lookup, she found phone numbers and started with Zenz and Franzen. Both calls went to voicemail and she left messages with them asking to speak about an issue that had come up involving Michael Tallon.

She figured that dropping the name would overcome the initial skepticism they were sure to exhibit.

Maitling, however, answered on the second ring. His voice was coarse and he sounded older than she'd imagined.

After introducing herself, Pauling brought up Michael Tallon's name.

"Tallon? Hell, yeah. Good guy. What's this about?" He spoke with a rapid-fire delivery. Like he was barking orders at her.

She decided to hedge just a little. "Well, I've been asked to investigate a criminal case that took place not long after you and Tallon took part in an operation in Turkey."

There was a long pause and Maitling didn't respond.

"I've got some questions about the operation and how they might have impacted my case." Having plowed ahead, Pauling was determined to force a response.

Finally, Maitling relented.

"Hold on while I make sure you are who you say you are."

Pauling listened as the sound of fingers working a keyboard resonated through the cell phone connection. He pounded the keys with a lot of force, much like the way he spoke.

She could hear Maitling breathing and it sounded a bit ragged. She wondered how old he was as that information was not provided in her search results. There was the possibility he wasn't in the greatest shape. Sometimes old soldiers had wounds that never healed.

A full two minutes went past before Maitling responded.

"Okay. I won't talk about it over the phone, though. Where are you?"

"I'm in New York. Manhattan."

She already knew where he was but didn't let on.

"Okay, I'm in Brooklyn and there's a coffee shop near my home. I go there every day at three for an espresso. If you want to meet me there and talk, great. If not, good luck."

His delivery was forceful and deadpan. Pauling felt like if she declined, he would hang up and seconds later never remember that they had even spoken. A black-and-white kind of guy, she was sure.

Pauling checked the clock and decided if she hurried she could make it there in time.

"Sounds good," Pauling said. "I could use a coffee."

CHAPTER TWENTY-SEVEN

For once, Tallon was happy for the traffic. Creeping along the freeway on the outskirts of Los Angeles was perfect. There was no way he could go more than ten miles per hour, what with the miles-long traffic jam he was sitting in.

Because of that, there was no way he could speed even if he wanted to, which he didn't. So there was absolutely no chance of getting pulled over by cops for any other reason than the officer wanting to reach his or her quota of tickets for the month.

So, Tallon waited patiently as the caravan of cars crept forward, eventually reaching the exit he was looking for after nearly an hour.

He descended into south central Los Angeles, and cruised until he found exactly what he was looking for: a busy convenience store with no sign of security cameras. The neighborhood was a bad one, home to the highest murder rate in the city.

Tallon pulled the SUV into the parking lot and gathered his backpack and duffel bag. He used an app on his phone to arrange a pickup at the taco stand he had passed a block away. He wasn't sure if the driver would object to picking him up in the ghetto, but the request went through.

When an alert came that his ride was less than a minute away, Tallon rolled down all of the windows in the SUV, left the keys in the ignition and walked away. He was sure it would be gone within the hour.

He walked past the convenience store and caught his ride; a young woman in a Hyundai sedan. She was white, with purple hair and a nose ring. Tallon thought she was quite pretty, and got a kick out of the utter fearlessness she showed at being in this part of LA.

"You're going to the W Hotel in Westwood?" she asked.

"That's the one," Tallon said.

"That'll be quite a change in scenery," the woman pointed out.

"Variety is the spice of life, they say."

"Yeah sell, this is beyond spicy. This is extra hot." She said it in a way that made it sound like a good thing.

She took surface streets and eventually they wound their way up to Westwood, a little suburban enclave just north of Santa Monica and home to the UCLA campus. Tallon tipped her and checked into his room, a suite overlooking a narrow street shaded by a row of gorgeous eucalyptus trees.

He'd thrown on a light jacket over his shirt, which he knew had bloodstains from the dead man he'd carried into the SUV. So now he went into the bathroom, removed the razor-sharp pocketknife from his pants, and took off all of his clothes. He carefully began to cut them into small, tiny pieces, tossing a handful of them at a time into the toilet, which he then flushed. He repeated the process nearly two dozen times until all of his clothes, and any DNA, were gone. He carefully washed and cleaned the pocketknife, and then took a long, scalding hot shower.

Retrieving clean clothes from the duffel bag, he dressed and grabbed a bottle of Heineken from the minibar.

When he felt the first few gulps of ice-cold beer hit his belly, and his muscles relax, he finally checked his phone.

Odd.

There were no new messages, save one.

It was from Peter Maitling asking him why a woman named Lauren Pauling wanted to talk to him.

Tallon's brow furrowed and he dialed Pauling's cell, but it went straight to voicemail.

As he drank his beer, he thought about how strange it was that Peter Maitling would contact him. He hadn't heard from Maitling in years. His nickname had been "Matey" even though he wasn't Australian – just a shortening of his surname.

Matey was a tough guy, one of the toughest Tallon had ever worked with. A westerner by birth, country strong as they say. Tallon remembered seeing Matey break the neck of a Taliban soldier with one hand.

As he drank his beer, Tallon began to have a bad feeling. He had only worked a few missions with Maitling, but one of them had been the one in southern Turkey. It was the very same op where Tallon had met Jessica Halbert.

Tallon shook his head.

First the email with Jessica's photo.

Then an ambush at his home.

And now a message from Maitling.

It was all connected and it was not good at all.

On the other hand, Lauren Pauling was involved.

That did more than just make Tallon confident his questions would eventually be answered.

It made him smile, too.

CHAPTER TWENTY-EIGHT

The melted cheese on the pizza reminded him of his face. As he pushed the pointed end of the slice of pepperoni into his mouth, he wondered if he should eat some of his own skin. Would it taste like cheese?

Probably not.

It was meat, after all. But it probably wouldn't taste like pepperoni. It'd be more gamey.

He laughed as he kept his eye on the coffee shop across the street. It occurred to him that he might be crazy. He used to think it all the time, especially when the nightmares took place in the day instead of just at night.

Waking up in sweat-soaked bedsheets in the middle of the night was one thing. Sitting in a chair at half past noon with your body shaking and ghosts of the past coming at you with knives was something else entirely.

There were days he couldn't remember who he was or what he'd done. One time he'd swum back into consciousness only to find himself stabbing a homeless man in the belly with an ice pick. The homeless man couldn't yell. He just kept groaning and letting out a small "oof" each time the ice pick was plunged into him.

The man still didn't think he was crazy, even as he realized he'd killed a homeless man for no reason. That it was reality, and not a nightmare.

It was only when he heard the term "disorganized killer" that he found his salvation. Indeed, he'd learned law enforcement often categorized murders into "organized" and "disorganized." They were terms, really, for premeditated crimes vs. crimes of passion, but the phrasing had really sunk in.

He'd been a bit disorganized, he'd realized.

Self-knowledge is so important in personal development. He'd read that in a book somewhere. It also applied to someone like him. A person who enjoyed killing and raping women, but also found pleasure in all acts of violence and homicide.

It was at that moment he put his true purpose together.

When he'd raped and murdered Jessica Halbert, he'd been freshly deranged and completely out of his mind. There had been some extenuating circumstances in that one, though, that made it different from all the others.

Looking back, it was astounding to him how under control he'd been during the murder. His mind had been in a constant state of frenzy back then, but somehow he had held it together well enough to get away with the crime and elude the authorities.

He'd really upped his game.

It was amazing, really.

Now he had at least a little bit of help, which he could have used back then. Like the information that some woman was going to be meeting with his old pal Peter Maitling.

Great.

He wondered if she was young or old. Would she be pretty? He'd just done a redhead. He secretly hoped she was a brunette or a fake blonde. He wondered what her skin was like. What her ass would taste like.

He giggled again and stuffed the rest of his pizza into his mouth.

Across the way, he watched as Peter Maitling stood up and extended his hand to a woman who had just arrived at the coffee shop. Maitling looked about the same, a short, powerful build with an air of no-nonsense about him. Except he didn't move as smoothly as he used to and his hair was gray.

The man across the street watched as Maitling waited for the woman to return with her coffee, which she did moments later.

He studied the woman closely.

Older than he ordinarily liked. Probably close to fifty. But she was really beautiful. A classic face and a nice body. Not a brunette, but light-haired, with maybe highlights. She held herself with confidence and had a nice trim body. A woman who clearly took good care of herself.

He would certainly enjoy killing and raping her. Maybe he'd do something special, get really creative with her.

What he saw before him was the epitome of what his killing strategy had become.

One victim for revenge.

One victim for pleasure.

He couldn't wait to get his hands on the woman across the street.

He wanted to hear her scream.

CHAPTER TWENTY-NINE

"Mr. Maitling?" Pauling asked. She had seen his picture on his driver's license from the database she'd used. She knew it was him. Plus, his voice was unmistakable. Like a machine gun firing bad ammo.

"Hey, you're good looking," he said. "I wasn't sure. Your voice sounds like you might be a bar fly."

Maitling was a short, powerful man who'd seen better days.

"What's wrong with being a bar fly?" Pauling responded, resisting the temptation to comment on the quality of *his* voice.

Maitling held up his hands as if to say he had no problem with it.

After getting her own coffee and returning to the table, she took the lead. Maitling didn't seem like the kind of guy who needed small talk, and Pauling wanted to get to the point.

"Thanks for meeting with me," she said. "So why weren't you comfortable speaking over the phone, Mr. Maitling?"

"Please. No one calls me mister. Call me Pete or Matey."

"Okay, Pete."

He smiled at her and raised an eyebrow. "How well do you know Tallon?"

"Quite well," she smiled back.

Maitling nodded. "Yeah, I figured. Frickin' Tallon always was good with the ladies. And, if you know him so well, you already know the answer to that question. The kind of work Tallon and I used to do is rarely talked about in public, certainly not over unsecured lines. That's a no-go."

"Used to?" Pauling asked. "Tallon's not really retired. Are you?"

Maitling nodded. "Sure am. Full medical disability, I won't go into the details. Let's just say I won't be jumping out of helicopters or sprinting up a mountain anytime soon."

Pauling had figured that already. She didn't know if it was some kind of long-term illness or the result of serious injury, but Maitling moved much slower than a man his age should. Plus, his breathing sounded labored.

He glanced down at his phone and gave an imperceptible nod. "Tallon says you're legit, but I already knew that."

Pauling had looked at her phone while she was ordering a coffee and saw that Tallon had called. She would have to call him back after this meeting was over.

"So ask away," Maitling said.

"Okay. I'm looking into the killing of Jessica Halbert," Pauling explained. "She was killed near the army base in Turkey not very long after your mission with Tallon, of which she was a part. I've been able to find almost nothing regarding what you were doing there and the reports are heavily censored."

"Yeah, of course."

"So what happened?"

"Am I missing something?" he asked. "Why do you think her death had anything to do with the mission? Maybe it was some boyfriend at the base she dumped. Or a psycho at the bar who came onto her and she shot down. Happens all the time. All it takes is one crazy bastard."

"Anything is possible," Pauling conceded. "But I didn't start here. I went through all of the files and reports from the original murder inquest performed by the army's special investigators. They couldn't find anyone who Halbert had rejected. No ex-boyfriends. No threats. No problems at all."

"I still don't get it."

"One name that did come up was Michael Tallon."

"Which would be expected."

"Sure. But let me share something else with you." Pauling led him through the process of how she had originally acquired the files. The arrival of the mysterious package, the reference to Reacher, her discovery of who the original investigator was. "So, ultimately, I connected the dots. I was chosen for a reason. And I think my relationship with Tallon was one of them. And the only thing that connects Tallon with Jessica Halbert is the mission you two shared. So that's why I'm asking."

Maitling nodded.

"Fair enough," he said. He took the smallish paper cup filled with espresso and tossed down the rest of the coffee. "Okay, I can't really get into too many specifics. All I can tell you is the mission was a classic smash and grab. Smash our way in, grab the guy we needed to, turn him over to an evacuation squad, gather whatever intel we could find, and leave."

He stopped there.

"Was the mission successful?"

"Of course. We were the best." He frowned at her like he was insulted by the question.

"Nothing happened with Jessica Halbert?"

"No. She was support at the launch phase. She didn't even come with us."

Pauling was puzzled by that response.

"Did anything happen during that phase? Anything out of the ordinary with her?"

"Nothing. Everything was smooth." Maitling held out a hand and slid it across the table horizontally to emphasize his point.

"How about when you got back?"

He shook his head. "Nope. We got back and it was all done like clockwork. The bad guy was taken away to be interrogated offsite. Evidence had been bagged and tagged. The team there catalogued everything, and we all went our separate ways."

Pauling studied the man across from her. As an FBI agent, she had interviewed many, many witnesses. She knew he wasn't lying to her, but she also knew that he wasn't telling her the whole story. He would be the kind of guy that would tell the truth, but he would put the onus on her to ask the right question.

"The mission itself went smoothly? No surprises?"

For the first time, he hesitated and she knew she'd asked the right question.

"We lost two men."

"Wait, out of four?"

"Five," Maitling said. "There were five of us."

Pauling immediately knew the files had been scrubbed even more thoroughly than she'd thought. Perhaps *doctored* would be the more appropriate term.

"You lost almost half your team and you called it a success?" Pauling let a tone of exasperation and skepticism creep into her voice.

"The mission was accomplished. Casualties happen." Maitling shrugged his considerable shoulders.

"How? How did they die?"

Again the hesitation. She was zeroing in on the thing he really didn't want to discuss.

"One died from gunshot wounds on the helicopter ride back to base. The other never made it out."

"What do you mean, never made it out?"

"He was captured by the locals."

"Michael Tallon left someone behind? Alive? I find that hard to believe."

"We didn't know he was still alive. We thought he was dead."

"That's a pretty big mistake."

Maitling let out a long, ragged breath. He crumpled the paper coffee cup in his hand and tossed it into a wastebasket a few feet away. When he turned back to Pauling, he leaned forward and put his elbows on the table.

"Zenz told us he was dead and there was no way we could go back and get his body," he growled at her. "Remember those scenes from Somalia? That's what it was like. There were hundreds of armed local militia. We barely made it out before air support arrived."

"Why did Zenz say the fifth man was dead if he wasn't?"

Maitling looked her directly in the eye. "I can only go so far with this, Ms. Pauling."

"Lauren."

"Here's what I can tell you, and it's all I can tell you." He put his phone in his pocket and leaned back in his chair. "Extended time in the bush can do things to a man. Everyone deals with it in their own way. Some guys work out like crazy. Others drink. Others retreat into themselves. Occasionally, some guys will use their time in the field as an escape. Do you know what I mean?"

"No."

"When you're an American soldier, backed by the most powerful army in the world, you feel like a god. Some of us accept the responsibility wisely. Others see it as an opportunity to let their basest instincts run wild. Now do you understand?"

Pauling was beginning to. "This fifth man was doing that? How?"

"Let's just say there was a 12-year-old local girl who lost her chance to be a 13-year-old in the worst way possible."

Pauling watched the movie play out in her mind. She was still missing something and then it clicked into place. "Zenz tried to stop him," she stated. "He was shot by the fifth man, and Zenz shot back. He thought he killed him and left him to die. But you guys have drones all over the place. You must have somehow learned he wasn't dead. The locals got him and discovered what he'd done to the young girl. Maybe even caught him in the act."

"Like I said," Maitling replied, holding out his hands in a helpless gesture. "I can only go so far and this is it."

"What was this man's name?"

Maitling just shook his head.

"And Jessica Halbert was nowhere near this?"

"No, ma'am."

It made no sense, Pauling thought.

She was still missing a key piece of the story.

She needed to talk to Michael Tallon.

CHAPTER THIRTY

The man sitting across the street watching Pauling and Maitling couldn't take his eyes off of the woman.

An older female like this Lauren Pauling was similar to the less desirable cuts of meat on a steer.

Not the filet mignon or the New York strip, but the tougher flank steak.

That's okay, he thought. Quite a bit could be done to enhance the flavor and perhaps tenderize her a bit.

Who knew, once he sunk his teeth into her he might enjoy the taste.

When she'd left, Maitling had waited a few minutes and then gone in the opposite direction, toward home.

The man across the street set aside his fantasies regarding Pauling. He decided first things first. He needed to take care of Maitling, who was a lot more cautious than Doug Franzen.

Maitling had taken care to meet Pauling in a public place, and continued to remain vigilant no matter where or what he was doing.

The man across the street had done his surveillance, however, and it had paid off.

When they'd served together, the man had remembered Maitling's distaste for doing laundry. Most of them did, but Maitling bitched about the chore constantly.

So now, once he'd started keeping tabs on his old comrade, he'd seen that Maitling always had his clothes laundered, and his shirts and pants dry cleaned.

It was always delivered on the same day at around the same time.

That consistency in a pattern was a sign that Maitling wasn't quite the soldier he used to be, or it was the one luxury he permitted himself.

In any event, it would be his downfall.

Now the man drove from the coffee shop and arrived at Maitling's apartment building just as Maitling went inside.

It was an older building from the 50s that had been well-maintained. He imagined the rooms were spacious and affordable for an ex-soldier surviving on a military pension and disability benefits.

He parked the car around the corner, put on surgical gloves, a white baseball cap like the laundry delivery person wore, and pulled two shirts on hangers wrapped in plastic from his trunk. He slid the short-barreled shotgun inside one of the shirts, and held it by the stock with the same hand that held the hangers.

He crossed the street and waited until a resident opened the door to Maitling's building and went inside.

Maitling lived on the second floor, so the man ducked into the stairwell, climbed the steps and made his way to the apartment with the number 209 marked on the door.

He gave a soft knock.

The man kept his face turned slightly downward so

Maitling could see both the baseball cap and the edge of the plastic hangers with the shirts.

He heard footsteps, a pause as the light changed beneath the gap between the bottom of the door and the floor. Sounds of two deadbolts being thrown and then the door creaked open.

The man lifted the shirts as if he was worried they were going to touch the floor, and as soon as the edge of Maitling's body was visible he fired the shotgun.

It was a 12 gauge. A model named the Mossberg Defender and the shells in the magazine were double-aught, designed to cut a man in half, which is what it did with Maitling.

The sound of the shotgun firing was obscenely loud. It sounded more like an explosion than gunfire.

The blast knocked Maitling onto his back, with most of his midsection blown apart. Blood was everywhere.

The man with the shotgun noted that Maitling had come to the door with a gun in his hand, just in case. But even then, he'd not been cautious enough.

Sloppy, he thought.

The man stepped into the apartment and swung the door shut behind him, although it didn't close correctly as jagged chunks of wood became caught in the doorjamb.

He walked forward and watched as Maitling's legs twitched and danced. He was trying to crawl away from his attacker, but nothing was working correctly.

The man took off his hat and with one hand, wiped some of the makeup off his face, so Maitling could see the scars.

"Remember me, Matey?" he laughed.

"You...bastard..." Maitling whispered. Blood gushed in a river of red as the dying man's heart pumped its last few beats.

"The sins of the past," the man said. He stepped over

Maitling, racked the pump of the shotgun and pointed the muzzle at Maitling's face. "Coming back to haunt you."

The light dimmed in Maitling's eyes and the man pulled the trigger, leaning his head slightly away to avoid the blowback.

When he turned to look at the damage, most of Maitling's head was gone. The stump of a neck oozed blood, chunks of flesh and bone were scattered across the floor.

The man was tempted to take a prize of sorts but realized he didn't have time, and the idea of framing Maitling for what would soon be Lauren Pauling's murder wouldn't make sense. He'd have to try to haul what was left of Maitling's body to Pauling's future crime scene, and that would be a mess.

Oh well.

He would leave the shotgun, though. Since it still had four more shells, he pumped it and shot up the remains of Maitling's body until there was nothing human recognizable and then tossed the shotgun into the middle of the room. The sound of the shotgun blasts echoed throughout the room and the man figured every single person in the building was on the phone calling 9-1-1.

He laid the shirts with their hangers on top of the main pool of blood.

"Now I see why you always hated doing laundry, Matey," the man said.

He lowered the baseball cap over his eyes and walked out of the dead man's apartment.

CHAPTER THIRTY-ONE

I n his hotel room in Los Angeles, Tallon read the details of Doug Franzen's suicide with something akin to disbelief.

Word of Franzen's untimely death had worked its way through the freelance grapevine eventually landing on Tallon's phone in the form of a text with a news link.

He'd clicked on it and read the disturbing news that Franzen, or "Franz" as they'd called him, was reported to have killed his girlfriend and then himself. Police had found the bodies in Franzen's truck. It seemed Franzen had killed his girlfriend in a frenzy, no pun intended, dismembering and mutilating the body.

Tallon had certainly known his fair share of men who'd come back home from the battlefield and been ticking time bombs. Good, brave, decent men who'd nonetheless been traumatized and psychologically damaged by what they'd seen and perhaps done overseas.

He'd even recently read a story where shockwaves from bomb blasts, including roadside bombs, could damage the brain much like the recent diagnosis of CTE, or brain damage, in professional football players. Those injuries had been linked to everything from depression and hallucinations to suicide and murder.

It was part of the unwritten contract of being a member of the military. You had to live what you'd gone through and sometimes, that wasn't an easy thing to do.

The problem was Tallon wasn't buying it in Franzen's case.

For one thing, he knew that physically, Franzen had taken part in a lot of missions and never been seriously injured. Certainly no damage to the head and brain. In fact, after he'd gotten out, Tallon remembered that Franzen joked about how invincible he was to have gone through so many tours of duty without serious injury.

Secondly, at one point Tallon had become Franzen's commanding officer and read his file. There was no sign of depression or anxiety. Not only was he a stable individual, Franzen had been one of the happiest, most positive and fun-loving members of their team.

Added to the mix was that Tallon had just seen Franzen less than a year ago. They'd gotten together in Virginia for beers and laughs. Franzen had been full of hopes and dreams. He'd met a girl and they were planning a family.

No, this whole thing stunk.

Especially in the context of two men showing up at Tallon's house to kill him.

Plus, the Halbert email.

And now this.

Doug Franzen.

It angered him. He went to his backpack, found his hand-gun, a 9mm, and made sure it was loaded. He crossed back to the couch, sat down and drank the rest of his beer.

Someone was going to pay for this.

All of it.

One way or another.

Tallon considered the flow of events. Jessica Halbert had been murdered in southern Turkey. Less than two days ago, someone had sent him a photo of her. Then a pair of hired killers had shown up and tried to murder him. Now here he was in Los Angeles reading about the death of one of the men who'd been with him on the operation that had included Halbert.

He thought long and hard about the plan of action ahead.

He could go back home, slip into a bunker mentality and wait for the next crew to come looking for him.

Kill them all one at a time.

Tallon immediately discarded that notion. It wasn't his style. He preferred to play offense and drive the action as opposed to adopting a passive approach. Sometimes, the conservative approach was the safer way to go, but in this case, Tallon didn't think it was.

The other option would be to fly to Virginia and start looking into what happened to Franzen himself. Cops didn't like civilians nosing around a murder-suicide investigation, but he knew a thing or two about working outside the wire. He could get some information and maybe deliver some justice, too.

He suddenly remembered Lauren Pauling had called him. He wondered what she wanted but instantly knew she was the perfect person to talk to. He could lay out some of what had happened, in general terms, and see what she thought. Maybe bounce a few ideas off her.

Just as he was reaching for his phone, it came to life with a new call.

Tallon glanced at the name.

Lauren Pauling.

CHAPTER THIRTY-TWO

J acobs was the first to arrive at the G & E Diversified Holding, Inc. storefront. He unlocked the front door and stepped inside. He went directly to the conference room, turned on the lights and started a pot of coffee. Soon, the aroma of fresh grounds permeated the office and would be the first thing Edgar smelled when he walked in the door. It would be comforting for him as the air outside was chilly, with a cold wind rattling the cheap, commercial-grade windows.

Jacobs waited and saw Edgar arrive first. He was always early to the meetings. Silvestri was always last. The older black man parked his SUV, locked it and walked to the building.

He opened the door and went straight to the conference room. He entered, nodded briefly to Jacobs and went straight for the coffee pot.

"Thanks for making this, we're going to need–"

He turned and saw Jacobs holding a gun with a long silencer on the end of it.

It was pointed directly at him.

"You–" Edgar began to say.

Jacobs pulled the trigger and the gun coughed.

A neat hole appeared in the middle of Edgar's forehead. Jacobs' gun spat again and Edgar fell backward, the fresh cup of coffee spilling onto his pressed white shirt as he crashed into the wall and slid down to the floor. The expression on his face never changed.

He'd looked disappointed.

Jacobs slid the pistol into the space behind his lower back and stepped out of the conference room, leaving the door slightly ajar.

The front door to the office opened again, and Silvestri stepped inside.

"Jesus, when did this cold front move in?" he asked.

"There's hot coffee in the room," Jacobs said. "I need to grab something from my car."

Silvestri nodded and walked past Jacobs. Jacobs moved like he was going to the front door but just as Silvestri passed him, he turned.

Later, Jacobs would be impressed with the man. Silvestri must have sensed something was wrong, some kind of hard-wired soldier's instinct. Or maybe when he didn't hear the door opening but instead heard Jacob's feet pivot, some deep recess in Silvestri's brain told him something bad was happening.

Silvestri lunged sideways but Jacobs had already drawn his gun and he fired twice.

The hair on the back of Silvestri's head puffed twice as two bullets entered the base of his skull. It was as if someone had blown two kisses at him, or the wind outside somehow made its way into the room.

Silvestri continued his move sideways and crashed to the floor, his thick, squat body landing with a thud and a soft bounce.

Jacobs worked quickly and dragged Silvestri into the conference room. He turned off the lights, and shut the door to the room, and then stepped outside, closed the outer door to the office and locked it, also setting the alarm system.

He hurried to his vehicle.

He didn't have much time.

He needed to reach Pauling before it was too late.

CHAPTER THIRTY-THREE

"Is Maitling legit?" Pauling asked Tallon. She was on her way home from the meeting with Maitling, her head still swimming with the information he'd provided. Pauling had immediately called Tallon to find out if she should believe what she'd just been told. She didn't have time for any bullshit. If what Maitling had told her was true, she finally had a sense of what was going on. If he was a crazy ex-merc, then she was back at square one.

"Of course he is," Tallon said. "The guy's one of the best in every sense of the word. "Why? Pauling, what the hell is going on?"

"It's going to take awhile to explain," she said. "Where are you?"

"In a hotel in Los Angeles."

"Why are you in a hotel in Los Angeles?"

"It would take awhile to explain," he said with a sigh. "Why don't you go first?"

"Okay." She took a deep breath and began with receiving the mysterious file on Jessica Halbert, seeing Reacher's name on the document, to finding Tallon's name also, and then putting two and two together in terms of the mission in southern Turkey being the common denominator.

He didn't question her line of logic. Instead, he asked, "So you were able to pin down Maitling and talk to him?"

"Yeah, and what he told me was crazy but it makes sense." She described the story of the fifth man who had apparently been in the process of raping or killing a young girl when he'd been discovered by Zenz. "Maybe Zenz stumbled into what he was doing to the young girl at the same time the girl's family did," Pauling said, trying out a theory. "No matter how it went down, you guys left him for dead."

"Well, technically Zenz did, but yeah, we all agreed it was the right decision," Tallon said, his voice taking on an edge. Pauling knew Tallon probably would have preferred to kill the man with his own hands."

"Who was this guy?"

Tallon laughed but it was utterly devoid of humor, instead colored by a caustic bitterness. "A real piece of shit named Leo Waters. There'd been rumors about his overzealousness with some of the locals. Including a mission where he disappeared for an hour or two. He was a really effective soldier, though. Vicious. Utterly without hesitation. Turned out, though, that violence was more than a career choice. It was in his soul, in a bad way."

"Wait a minute," Pauling said. "Does all of this have to do with why you're in LA? It's your turn. Tell me what's going on."

Tallon told her about the mysterious email with Halbert's photo, the news that it most likely came from within the army's firewalls, and then the arrival of two men who wanted to have a word with him. "Ultimately, they decided to spend some time in the desert, just the two of them, and asked me to drive their vehicle to LA for them."

There was a silence as Pauling processed the real meaning of his words.

"I see," she said.

"That's not all, though," Tallon continued. He told her about the news of Doug Franzen's murder and suicide. He finished by saying, "I don't believe in coincidences. I find it hard to believe that two men tried to kill me, someone killed Franzen's girlfriend and maybe it wasn't a suicide, and now you're having a secret meeting with Maitling. It's all connected."

"You think Leo Waters survived?" Pauling said. "You guys said Zenz was sure he was dead. If the locals knew he was raping one of their young women, they would have killed him. They don't mess around in Syria with that kind of thing."

"We called in air support, though," Tallon said. "It's not completely out of the realm of possibility. If he was still alive when the bombs were dropped, I suppose there's a chance he could have escaped in the confusion. If he hadn't been dead already, of course."

"In which case, he might have revenge on his mind."

"And since he's a rapist, he could have raped Franzen's girlfriend, killed Franzen and arranged it to look like a murder-suicide," Tallon ventured. "It would be just the kind of sick, twisted plan Waters would come up with. It would serve two purposes for him."

"Or maybe he framed Franzen for the murder hoping he'd commit suicide," Pauling said. "Same result, either way."

"Yeah," Tallon said.

Pauling heard the anger in his voice and considered the new information for a moment. "But is this Leo Waters powerful enough to hire two killers to take you out? Does he have that kind of money?"

"No, I doubt it," Tallon said.

"Then who?"

"I don't know."

"But you're still in danger," Pauling said. "Waters is out there looking for you."

"He's looking for Maitling, too."

"And Zenz."

"Zenz is dead," Tallon said. "He died of cancer last year."

Pauling made an executive decision.

"I'm getting you the first direct flight from LA to New York. You can be here in six hours."

"We need to find Waters as soon as possible," Tallon said. "And stop him. Once and for all."

CHAPTER THIRTY-FOUR

They met at a safe house Jacobs paid for through a variety of shell companies, some involved with the military and some not. Key, however, was that part of the trail wound its way right back into the Department of Defense.

The government's own firewalls were some of the most impressive in the world. Any investigation there would stall, unless it came from within. And if that were the case, Jacobs would know about it.

He watched as Leo Waters entered the front door and locked the doors behind him. The safe house was a duplex in a low-rent neighborhood full of people *in transition* as the social workers liked to say. Both sides of the duplex were vacant, but someone from Jacobs' office occasionally spent the weekend there to make it look occupied. They also collected the mail and made sure the place wasn't overrun with pests or local vandals.

The best thing about the safe house, and the reason Jacobs had chosen it for this meeting with Waters, was that it was the kind of place where strange faces meant nothing. The population was mostly transient and there was plenty of turn over, so even a face as bizarre as Waters' wouldn't be remembered.

Jacobs watched as Waters went into the living room and dropped into a chair.

As usual, Jacobs had a hard time looking directly at the man. His deformities were fairly well concealed, but their shared history made it difficult for Jacobs to look him in the eye.

"Three down, one to go," Waters said. "Matey is kinda dead-y."

The grotesque shell of a man began laughing and Jacobs fought down a bout of revulsion.

"I'm sure you made it as messy as possible so the police will be extra motivated." Jacobs had urged Waters to make the murders look like accidents, much the way he'd done with the original Army investigator Thomas Wainwright.

"Hey, that's your problem," Waters replied. "I make the messes, you clean them up. It's what makes our partnership work. Everyone has a role and they know what it is."

"Great," Jacobs replied.

"Hey, you made the first mess, so don't put this all on me."

"What the hell is that supposed to mean?" Jacobs fired back.

"It means if you hadn't gotten so pissed when Jessica Halbert rejected you, none of this would have happened," Waters said. A lopsided, ghastly grin covered his face. "You raped and killed her–"

"You were right there with me, don't act all innocent."

"–and then tried to blame me for it, which was a real piece-of-shit move."

"I didn't blame you," Jacobs replied. "Besides, you were the one who did most of the raping."

"We tag teamed her and I think you loved it more than I

did," Waters said. "She wasn't my first, but she was yours, right?"

Jacobs sat in a chair across from Waters. The furniture in the safe house had been bought secondhand from a Salvation Army store. Same with the horrendous artwork on display. One of them was a paint-by-numbers Jacobs noticed.

"How many others were there?" he finally asked Waters. He'd always wondered just how evil the man was he'd chosen to join forces with. At the time, it was really his only option.

"Lots."

"That's what I thought."

"So when Zenz left me to die in that shithole, you were secretly happy," Waters continued. His voice was calm but filled with venomous animosity. "Until I got word to you that I'd survived, and had plenty of evidence tying you to Halbert's murder so you'd better help a brother out."

Waters laughed hard.

"Oh, I'm going to help you out, all right," Jacobs said.

He swung the pistol he'd been holding behind his back and fired at Waters. But Waters had seen it coming and torqued his body off the chair onto the floor, firing as he went.

Jacobs' bullets plowed into Waters' left side, shattering his left elbow and embedding itself in his shoulder.

Waters jackknifed forward and kept firing back at Jacobs. When his elbows hit the floor it forced his pistol up and his first shot went high, missing altogether. In a flash, he readjusted his aim and fired again, just before the bullets from Jacobs ruined his left arm.

Waters' second shot didn't miss.

It caught Jacobs just underneath the point of his chin and it plowed up through his mouth, cratering his palate and blowing out the back of his brain.

Jacobs' body went slack and he slumped to the floor.

Waters sat up and looked into Jacobs' lifeless eyes.

It took a minute for him to realize how badly he'd been hit. His left arm was useless, his elbow was a mess and his shoulder wouldn't move.

Even worse, Jacobs had also shot him in the right hip, a devastating blow that had certainly cracked bone and dug a deep furrow through his flesh. Parts of his body were completely unresponsive and he struggled to get to his feet.

"You miserable piece of shit," Waters said to the lifeless body of Jacobs. Waters emptied the rest of the clip in his pistol into Jacobs. The bullets smacked into the corpse and the sound reverberated in the room.

Waters staggered to his feet and retrieved Jacobs' phone. He saw the last message. It was from someone on Jacobs' staff and it showed an intercepted message relaying that a flight had been booked for Michael Tallon to New York. It showed Tallon's arrival time at LaGuardia.

Waters knew Lauren Pauling would pick him up and he checked his watch. The timing would work perfectly.

It was time for the final act.

Get rid of Tallon.

Rape and kill Pauling.

Maybe disappear for awhile.

Stranger things had been known to happen.

CHAPTER THIRTY-FIVE

Pauling returned to her condo and had the building's valet bring around her car. She rarely drove in the city, but occasionally she needed transportation beyond cabs or Ubers. Her ride of choice was a Range Rover and it was kept in the building's basement garage, sometimes sitting there for months on end, unused.

It would take a few minutes for the valet to bring the Rover around, so Pauling took the opportunity to go to her condo to retrieve her iPad. She'd already downloaded the case files onto it and while she waited for Tallon, she could revisit them in light of the new information she'd received.

Back downstairs, she tipped the valet and climbed into the Rover, and fought traffic all the way out to the cell phone lot at LaGuardia. She parked, and read all of the horrible news stories about the murder-suicide of Doug Franzen and his girlfriend, Dawn Fitzgerald.

Tallon had forwarded her the links.

The killing was beyond gruesome. It sounded like a vicious rape, perhaps drug-and-alcohol-induced. The autopsies would reveal more, but Pauling already had her suspicions and they had to do with Leo Waters. The name had been a surprise to her and she tried to remember if she'd seen the name in the case files from the Halbert murder. She was sure there had been no mention of him.

Or had there?

Pauling dug out her iPad and searched back through the files.

If Leo Waters had actually survived, how had he done it? He'd been caught committing a horrific crime by enemies of the U.S., and his own army had left him behind, committing him to a swift and certain death.

But somehow, he may have survived.

And started killing.

Or, perhaps he had continued to kill, picking up where he'd left off. If he'd been in his late twenties in the army, there might be more transgressions in his past. Serial killers often began working out their demons quite young. Starting with the torture of animals. Working their way up to assault, then rape, and finally murder.

So what had happened when he'd returned, if he made it back? How did he survive? And where did he show up? The army base in Turkey? Or had he somehow gone in a different direction, deeper into Syria?

Wouldn't people have spotted him as an American soldier? Were there even friendly allies in the area at that time?

She dug through the files some more.

There was nothing. She couldn't find anything to shed light on the Leo Waters mystery.

As she glanced at her phone, a news bulletin appeared describing the discovery of two men in a suburb of Washington, D.C. Both of them were decorated military veterans and they had been murdered.

Their last names were Edgar and Silvestri.

Pauling's breath caught in her throat.

Those names were in the report, along with a man named Jacobs. If she recalled correctly, they hadn't been actively involved in the mission, but she'd seen their names nonetheless. Maybe as part of the support team on the mission? Or had their names been in the homicide file?

Jesus Christ, she really needed to talk to Tallon in person.

It seemed to take ages before he finally texted that he had landed and it took another twenty minutes before he finally emerged near the baggage claim. He looked the same as always to Pauling; handsome, capable, and smiling.

He hopped into Pauling's Range Rover and she spirited him away from the airport.

"You look good," he said. "Thanks for picking me up."

"You too," she answered. There would be plenty of time for them to get reacquainted later. Right now, she needed answers. "Edgar, Silvestri and Jacobs."

"The big three," Tallon said. "They ran a lot of major operations back in the day. Rumor was Jacobs had more to do with the CIA than the military. But that was just a rumor. I never really worked with them, though, and certainly not on the mission with Halbert. Why do you mention them?"

"Because Silvestri and Edgar are dead. Murdered. This morning. According to what I read, their wives used GPS to track down their phones and vehicles. Found them at some fake business in a strip mall outside D.C.

"A CIA front, no doubt," Tallon pointed out. "I wonder if Jacobs was involved."

"Or Leo Waters."

"Yeah, goddamned Leo Waters."

"Why don't you tell me about him?" Pauling wound her way through traffic, heading back to Manhattan and her condo.

"I already did tell you what I know. The veneer of an excellent soldier over the soul of a psychopath. There's more than one in this man's army," Tallon said. "They're tough to see, sometimes. Especially when the fog of war sets in."

Pauling enjoyed hearing the sound of Tallon's voice. He smelled nice, too.

"Where was Waters originally from?" she asked.

"Who knows? I never knew anything more about him. He was just another guy."

"We'll have to go back to my place and research him. Maybe I can find some files on him like I did these," she said, gesturing toward her iPad on the seat between them.

Tallon looked out the window of the Rover into the darkness of the night. "It just doesn't make sense. It was impossible for him to survive. There's no way he could make it out of Syria alone, and we never heard a word from any other units they'd found one of our guys."

"Would they do that?"

"Hell, yeah. You rescue a guy from a unit, one of the first things you do is send word to that unit. We never heard a word. Which means he wasn't picked up by any friendlies."

"So how'd he make it back?"

"He would have had to have gotten help. No other way."

"When you say 'our guys,' who do you mean?"

"At that time, army guys. It was an army op, mostly."

"What if he'd gotten help from friendlies, just not *your* friendlies?" Pauling asked.

"Who do you mean?"

"What you said about Jacobs," she answered. "CIA."

Tallon turned in his seat and looked at her. He nodded.

"Yeah, that could have been what happened. If the spooks picked him, they probably wouldn't have told us. That's how they work."

Pauling thought they might be onto something.

"Yeah, those CIA creeps," Tallon said. "I wouldn't be surprised."

CHAPTER THIRTY-SIX

W aters had to marvel at his partner's efficiency. Not only had he quickly figured out how to plan to kill him, Jacobs had even put together a quick op for Pauling and Tallon.

He felt a grudging respect for the man he'd just killed.

Even though that man had put several bullets into him and was causing him a great deal of pain and blood loss at the moment.

Waters giggled. He felt a little lightheaded and dizzy, but he still felt good. He was excited.

He couldn't wait to get his hands on Pauling.

He would have to do it without Jacobs, though. He thought again of his silent partner in crime. It must have been difficult for Jacobs, Waters reasoned. Pretending to be a part of the team that included Edgar and Silvestri, who were obsessed with tracking down the escaped and crazed Leo Waters.

When in actuality, Jacobs hadn't been trying to find Waters at all. He'd actually been working to prevent the others from finding him. He'd been acting all along, pretending to be frustrated with each disaster as it unfolded, while actively supporting the debacles.

All because of sweet Jessica Halbert, Waters remembered.

Jacobs, a young, arrogant officer had been soundly rejected by the beautiful young woman and had temporarily blacked out with rage.

Waters, his drinking buddy, had seen an opportunity. He, himself, was already on his way to becoming a full-fledged killer of women. So when he got his hands dirty with Jacobs, he knew it would work out to his benefit. Together, they'd abducted Halbert and taken her out into the woods and had their fun. Truth be told, he, Waters, had had a lot more fun. Jacobs had been a newbie, and mostly watched.

Waters had been advanced enough to know that he'd just implicated his buddy, who was in a higher position and on a much faster path to advancement. He knew it would come in handy one day.

And it sure did.

Rather quickly, at that.

He thought back to that day in Syria.

The bad guy who was the target of the mission had been caught and the extraction had happened quickly and smoothly. The rest of them were then tasked with finding and gathering any additional intelligence.

Waters remembered how when he burst into a bedroom in the house he was searching, he came face-to-face with the most stunning Arab girl he'd ever seen in his life.

She was that glorious pre-pubescent age.

Perfect skin.

The beginning of a woman's curves.

Unspoiled.

He'd locked the door, slapped a piece of tape across her mouth and raped her. All the time, the family had been pounding on the door, trying to get in and see what the bad American was doing to their daughter.

He was on top of the girl, thrusting himself into her lifeless body with his hands around her throat, when Zenz had crashed through the door.

The rest of the family had spilled through, too. The mother collapsed, screaming, the father and two sons attacked Waters, punching and hitting him, pinning his arms before he could get to his weapons.

More men streamed into the room and he saw out of the corner of his eye as Zenz disappeared around the doorway and out of harm's way.

His fellow soldier had abandoned him.

All because he was getting laid while on the job.

Eventually, the family and insane villagers had dragged Waters down to the courtyard where a fire had been started. It seemed like the whole tiny community appeared with knives and clubs, all intent on beating him to death. They began to literally tear him apart.

And then the bombs had fallen and just like that, he was free.

Punishment served.

He stole the truck, drove all the way back into Syria, where his partner in crime, Jacobs, arranged for his rescue and medical care using a secret CIA plane and personnel.

It took him nearly a year to recover from the vicious wounds and savage beating.

Once he was healthy and able, he began to kill again.

Waters smiled at the memories as he waited outside Pauling's building. According to Jacobs' file, the woman had an intense security system, which meant he needed to take them out on the street.

Preferably, Tallon would go first, and then he could force

the woman up to her apartment, where he would satisfy himself and then cut her into ribbons.

He looked down at his own wounds and saw the amount of blood he was losing.

Waters laughed again.

He didn't have much time.

CHAPTER THIRTY-SEVEN

A light rain had begun to fall as Pauling maneuvered the Range Rover up 4th Street. Traffic hadn't been bad at this time of night, and they'd made good time.

They pulled up to the building and the valet came out. He was carrying a small umbrella and wore a black jacket. A ring of car keys dangled from his belt loop as he approached the passenger side door.

Pauling gathered her purse and iPad from the seat between herself and Tallon, while he reached back into the vehicle and grabbed his backpack and duffel bag. He was looking forward to getting to the bottom of this mess and being able to reunite with Pauling in the way he most enjoyed.

A smile formed on his face as he began to turn back. He was going to say something to Pauling when the image of the parking valet snagged in his mind.

It was the man's shoes.

Time slowed to a crawl as the image flashed through Tallon's mind. He saw the shoes and they weren't really shoes.

They were beige hiking boots, totally at odds with the black jacket, and reminded him of military footwear.

His motion came to an abrupt stop and he reversed his energy, throwing himself backward into the rear of the vehicle.

Gunfire erupted and glass shattered all around Tallon. He felt something tear into his chest and legs.

Waters.

Tallon dove deeper into the rear of the SUV. He'd been unable to bring his guns on the plane from Los Angeles, so he was unarmed.

Tallon also instinctively knew that he was the primary target, and that Waters would want Pauling for last. It was why he'd attacked them on the passenger side and chosen to disguise himself as the valet. Because he wanted to get to Tallon first.

Tallon belly crawled into the back seat and dove for the opposite rear door, directly behind the driver. He managed to unlock it and spill out of the Range Rover onto the wet pavement.

Behind him, he heard more gunfire, followed by the sound of glass shattering and bullets smashing into metal.

Tallon knew he'd been shot, but he didn't know where.

And there was no time to check his wounds.

Waters was coming for him.

CHAPTER THIRTY-EIGHT

P auling had just stepped out of the vehicle when the first series of shots punched through the Rover.

She knew without hesitation that Waters had pretended to be the valet so he could get close and open fire. Pauling also recognized the gun.

It was an automatic weapon.

So she was outgunned.

She also knew Waters had targeted Tallon first. Maybe because Tallon was the more formidable opponent, or because he wanted Pauling for more than just murder.

She withdrew her gun from its shoulder holster in one swift, smooth motion, dropping her purse and iPad in the process. Using the hood of the vehicle as cover, she took aim at Waters.

But he wasn't there.

Behind her, she heard Tallon hit the ground.

Pauling's mind processed the options for Waters: come around the front of the vehicle, around the back, or over the top.

In less than a full second, she quickly worked through the probabilities, immediately eliminating the first.

He was not coming around the front.

The rear approach would be expected and also provided him the most cover.

Because it was the obvious choice, she guessed he would avoid it.

And when Pauling felt the Range Rover's body rock imperceptibly, she knew that something of significant weight had caused it to shift.

And, she knew she was right.

Pauling immediately raised her firearm and pointed it at the roof of the Rover, just above the rear passenger door.

As her gun came on line, a face filled with hatred and rage appeared and without hesitating, Pauling pulled the trigger, firing a three-shot burst in less than a second.

She caught him just as he was taking aim at Tallon.

Her first bullet caught him at the hairline and a piece of scalp popped from his skull. Pauling knew her next two rounds were just as accurate, but she hadn't seen where they'd hit.

Waters' face disappeared from view and the Rover shifted again.

Pauling heard the body hit the pavement on the other side.

She ducked around the front of the vehicle, her gun held in front of her with two hands.

Waters was on the ground, rolling onto his side. He still had his weapon, a short-barreled submachine gun, clenched in his blood-covered hands.

The rain had begun to fall harder and Pauling saw the scar tissue on the man's face, noted the blood all over the front of his clothes and she realized he'd been shot by someone else, before he'd attacked them.

Waters was trying to bring the submachine gun to bear on Pauling so she fired five times in rapid succession, punching bullets into his sternum, and one into his forehead, inches below her first shot.

Waters collapsed back onto the wet pavement. The submachine gun clattered to the ground and Waters' hands were pointed toward the sky, his fingers extended like claws.

His body was crooked, as if his hips were knocked out of place.

He was dead.

There was moaning, but it wasn't coming from Waters.

It was Tallon.

CHAPTER THIRTY-NINE

I t had been a little over a week since Leo Waters had attacked them outside Pauling's building.

Tallon had been treated for one gunshot wound. The bullet had grazed a rib but hadn't broken it, and careened off into the night, carrying with it only a small amount of flesh and muscle.

Tallon had also suffered superficial cuts to his face and body from the exploding glass. They were small, however, and wouldn't require stitches.

He had been treated and released from the hospital after two days.

They received visits from the police, FBI and the army, as well as several government agents who offered no specific affiliations with an organization.

Pauling shared everything she had, withholding only the admission that she had private access to the FBI's servers. Instead, she had implied she had received all of the information from the deceased military investigator, Thomas Wainwright.

The visitor from the army confirmed that Wainwright had been given the nickname Reacher Jr. for his physical resemblance to the original legendary special investigator.

The same official had stated that Wainwright had done his homework on Reacher, and must have found out about Pauling's connection with him.

Seeing the case as either a dead end, or recognized that progress in the Halbert case required help outside the system, he had sent the files to Pauling, implying they were from Reacher in order to overcome any reluctance she might have to getting involved.

When the last interview was finished, and the last quiet man who asked questions but offered nothing in return had left, Pauling poured a glass of wine for herself and an expensive glass of scotch for Tallon.

They were in her living room, Tallon still sporting bandages from their encounter with Waters. Candles were lit and the sky, visible through the living room's large windows, was a dark purple, streaked with jagged ribbons of light gray clouds. Above them, the stars would soon appear.

"I'm still not sure who was crazier, Jacobs or Waters," Tallon said. "One's insanity was obvious, the other one hid it well."

"In some ways Jacobs was the more dangerous because of that," Pauling said. "It allowed him to get into positions of power. The kind that Waters could never achieve."

They sat in silence for a moment, still digesting everything that had happened. The incredible amount of death and tragedy Waters and Jacobs had caused.

Pauling had brought in a piece of paper from her office and it was now on the couch next to her. She glanced at it and Tallon followed her gaze.

"More paperwork from them?" he asked. "Jesus, I've

signed so many releases and statements my wrist is hurting more than my gunshot wound."

Pauling laughed. "No, this isn't anything to do with the case."

He sensed there was more to it. Pauling's fabulous, husky voice had grown softer. She had a mysterious expression on her face and Tallon thought she had never looked more beautiful than she did right then.

He savored the vision of her and then asked, "Come on, what gives?"

She smiled at him.

"Do you remember awhile back asking me about maybe making our relationship a little more consistent?"

He laughed. "Consistent? Doesn't sound like a word I would use, but okay. Yeah, I remember the conversation. It was fairly one-sided as I recall." He raised an eyebrow, letting her know that he'd made the offer, but she hadn't responded.

"My signature on this piece of paper would be a step in that direction," she said.

"What is it? A pre-nup?" he asked, a smile on his face.

Pauling laughed and handed the sheet of paper to Tallon. He read it over and then let out a long, low whistle.

"Holy cow, I would be a kept man."

"You're a keeper, I'll admit that," Pauling said. "This is just a step. I'm still going to work cases, but they're going to be fewer and only ones in which I'm really interested. Pro bono, actually. But without the hassle of running my own company. Which means I'll have more time for other things."

"Like what?" he asked.

She signed the paper with a flourish and focused her green-eyed gaze on Tallon.

"Like you."

. . .

THE END

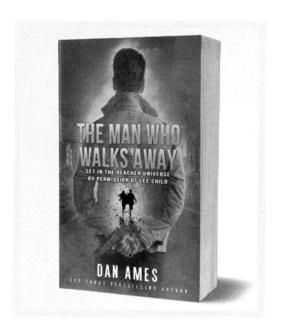

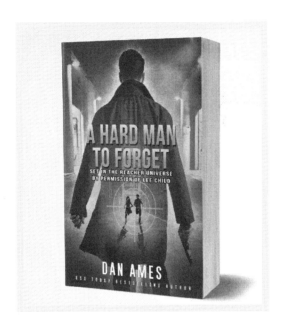

Book One in The JACK REACHER Cases

BOOK ONE IN A THRILLING NEW SERIES

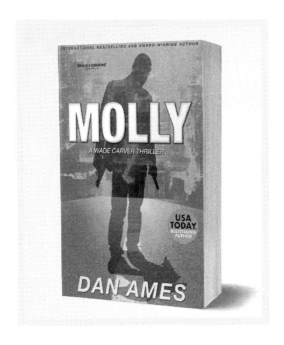

A Blazing Hot New Mystery Thriller Series!

ALSO BY DAN AMES

The JACK REACHER Cases #1 (A Hard Man To Forget)

The JACK REACHER Cases #2 (The Right Man For Revenge)

The JACK REACHER Cases #3 (A Man Made For Killing)

The JACK REACHER Cases #4 (The Last Man To Murder)

The JACK REACHER Cases #5 (The Man With No Mercy)

The JACK REACHER Cases #6 (A Man Out For Blood)

The Jack Reacher Cases #7 (A Man Beyond The Law)

The JACK REACHER Cases #8 (The Man Who Walks Away)

DEAD WOOD (John Rockne Mystery #1)

HARD ROCK (John Rockne Mystery #2)

COLD JADE (John Rockne Mystery #3)

LONG SHOT (John Rockne Mystery #4)

EASY PREY (John Rockne Mystery #5)

BODY BLOW (John Rockne Mystery #6)

MOLLY (Wade Carver Thriller #1)

SUGAR (Wade Carver Thriller #2)

ANGEL (Wade Carver Thriller #3)

THE KILLING LEAGUE (Wallace Mack Thriller #1)

THE MURDER STORE (Wallace Mack Thriller #2)

FINDERS KILLERS (Wallace Mack Thriller #3)

DEATH BY SARCASM (Mary Cooper Mystery #1)

MURDER WITH SARCASTIC INTENT (Mary Cooper Mystery #2)

GROSS SARCASTIC HOMICIDE (Mary Cooper Mystery #3)

KILLER GROOVE (Rockne & Cooper Mystery #1)

BEER MONEY (Burr Ashland Mystery #1)

THE CIRCUIT RIDER (Circuit Rider #1)

KILLER'S DRAW (Circuit Rider #2)

TO FIND A MOUNTAIN (A WWII Thriller)

STANDALONE THRILLERS:

THE RECRUITER

KILLING THE RAT

HEAD SHOT

THE BUTCHER

BOX SETS:

AMES TO KILL

GROSSE POINTE PULP

GROSSE POINTE PULP 2

TOTAL SARCASM

WALLACE MACK THRILLER COLLECTION

SHORT STORIES:

THE GARBAGE COLLECTOR

BULLET RIVER

SCHOOL GIRL

HANGING CURVE

SCALE OF JUSTICE

ABOUT THE AUTHOR

Dan Ames is a USA TODAY Bestselling Author, Amazon Kindle #1 bestseller and winner of the Independent Book Award for Crime Fiction.

www.authordanames.com
dan@authordanames.com

Made in the USA
Columbia, SC
29 January 2021